Bazooka Town – Spring 1945: D

By

Sergeant Robert Lofthouse

Copyright Robert Lofthouse 2014.

To all who suffered and endured during those dark times, 1939-1945.

'Only the dead have seen the end of war.'
Plato

Foreword by Major Justin Featherstone MC

The narrative of war places a stark and often disquieting lens on the tensions between social identity and humanity. In 'Bazooka Town', Robert Lofthouse again uses his deep personal insight as a former infantry Sergeant and combat veteran to create the carefully-crafted characters at the heart of this irregular band of guerrilla fighters operating in the deepening shadows of the final stages of the war in Europe. It would have been too easy to draw the individual partisans in an overly-simplistic manner, making Erik an innocent, and guerrilla leader Dieter grotesque, but the author avoids such binary and unchallenging images.

The original Operation Werewolf led to the training of a commando force by Obergruppenführer Prützmann, which by early 1945 comprised of probably no more than two hundred soldiers, largely drawn from the Hitler Jugend. This largely ineffectual organisation was more of a propaganda tool, and proved of no subsequent military significance, but Dieter's band would have drawn inspiration from Joseph Goebbels' 'Werewolf Speech' of 23rd March 1945, in which he called for all native Germans to fight to the death, in a demonstration of resistance to the advancing Allied armies.

It is against this historical backdrop that the author sets Erik's journey from his hastened recruit training on the Senne, to his family's faltering steps of recovery and rediscovery in the shattered post-war Paderborn community. Erik's experiences of fighting resonate deeply, from the initial tank ambush at Kirchborchen to the final battle at a roadblock, and reflect the confusion, horror, desperation and intimacy of close combat. From the meticulous and enervating preparation at the ambush site around the roadblock, through the shock of encountering an armoured advance, to the percussion effects of the stick grenades thrown by the partisans, the reader is propelled in to the maelstrom, and it is possible to feel that you are genuinely at the side of this young soldier.

The escalation of partisan activity from ambushes and close-quarter assassinations, to the murder of civilians and the abhorrent treatment of prisoners, is both shocking and rapid. The question of why essentially good men can become so morally degenerate is at the core of this book.

'Bazooka Town' is multi-layered, relentless, relevant and powerful. As a detailed and rigorously related narrative of a broken irregular unit fighting a desperate and futile insurgent action, it is both dramatic and engrossing. As a study of the insidious impact on moral agency by social identity and social structure, it is even more deeply affecting. The dehumanisation of Dieter and his sidekick second-in-command Thomas, and their transition from regular soldiers to brigands capable of acts of barbarism, provokes moral outrage. This erosion of humanity is even more marked as witnessed by Erik, who although traumatised, resists the corrupting effect of what the others view as an existential fight. For the other Werewolves, national survival and dignity are causes that supercede the accepted conventions of both war and morality; the attrition caused by the years of fighting within a Total War environment have led to them losing the touchstones of perceived decency and sense of self.

Erik's final encounter represents this clash of a sacrosanct, incorrigible moral core, depicted by the warmth of a patriarchal panzer commanding officer, and the resolute adherence to an ideology and desire for survival that eclipses all governed and rational behaviours, both on and away from the field of battle. It is this very idea that remains the foundation of professional military ethos and discipline; as much to protect the mental wellbeing of individual soldiers, as to prevent acts of inhumanity in an environment where humanity itself remains so fragile.

This nuanced and arresting portrait of the tensions between a soldier's sense of self, agency, identity and morality, is framed with integrity, and a genuine understanding that can only come from a soldier's heart. These ideas remain as conflicted and tested today in modern military operations, as in 1945, in which the events are set.

Major Justin Featherstone MC

AUTHOR'S NOTE

Officially, open hostilities between Allied and the German armed forces ended on 7th May 1945. You would be forgiven to think that as far as the European Theatre of Operations was concerned, the war was over. Only for the majority was this true. The continued resistance of certain German forces in fact continued well beyond 1945.

Not unlike what coalition forces faced in both Iraq and Afghanistan recently, the Allied occupying forces faced a grave threat from certain insurgent factions comprising of pro-Nazi citizens, Waffen SS, Hitler Youth, and a small number of Werhmacht, Kriegsmarine and Luftwaffe personnel. Despite the formal surrender of the German armed forces on 7th May, there were many small groups who ignored the declaration and continued to fight on regardless. Radio communications in April–May 1945 were limited at best between German command locations and their fighting units.

Heinrich Himmler, leader of the SS, considered the possibility of an insurgent force operating behind enemy lines, as the Allies occupied Germany itself. Himmler was without ceremony berated by Hitler for considering such an idea. In Hitler's mind, to promote an insurgency was to admit his armed forces were losing. He dismissed Himmler's idea out of hand, and would not discuss it any further. Without the blessing of the

Fuhrer, Himmler raised a guerrilla army of Nazi diehards. Their role would be to allow the enemy to occupy Germany, and then to cause trouble from within; killing enemy soldiers not mindful of their personal security, murdering German citizens seen to collaborate with the invaders. The codename given to this band of brigands was 'Werewolf'.

Joseph Goebbels came onside with the idea, and promoted Radio Werewolf, a pirate radio station designed to win over the German public, and also instruct them on how to use the standard infantry weapons of the German army. The broadcasts enjoyed a limited element of success; citizens rising up, ambushing couriers or outriders, disrupting rail links of Allied supply. There was Werewolf success in the assassination of newly-elected officials of German towns and cities, puppet politicians put in place by the occupying forces.

Werewolf actions throughout Germany were more of a nuisance than a real sting in the side of the Allies. The British were subject to some Werewolf activity in the early years of occupation, but the Americans and Russians took the brunt of the actions up to the mid-1950s.

The Werewolves knew the Russians were not shy in carrying out reprisals for attacks on their supply convoys, and that the reprisals would achieve nothing more than swell Werewolf ranks in the Soviet zone. But for the majority of

Germans, the uprising never really materialised, Werewolf activity generally diminishing from violent acts to passive acts of non-compliance; not cooperating with new laws and guidelines frustrated the Allies for a while, but before long, even passive acts became weary, those opposing the occupation merely falling in line.

But as devil's advocate, regardless of who started the war; if your country was invaded, what would you do?

Surrender? Collaborate? Or resist?

Sergeant Robert Lofthouse.

TABLE OF CONTENTS

Foreword by Major Justin Featherstone MC   1
Author's Note   5

Prologue: Ambush at Kirchborchen   9

Part One: The Battle
    Chapter One – The March   13
    Chapter Two – The Master Bedroom   21
    Chapter Three – Tank Assault   33
    Chapter Four – War Crimes   48
    Chapter Five – Second Shove   56
    Chapter Six – Retreat to Paderborn   65
    Chapter Seven – Retreat to Schlangen   81

Part Two: The Werewolves
    Chapter Eight – The Farmhouse   93
    Chapter Nine – Deserters and Insurgents   103
    Chapter Ten – The Roadblock   115
    Chapter Eleven – Night Raid   124
    Chapter Twelve – The Party   134
    Chapter Thirteen – Backlash   157
    Chapter Fourteen – Rearguard Action   172
    Chapter Fifteen – The Pied Piper   191
    Chapter Sixteen – Horn   207
    Chapter Seventeen – The End of the Road   221

Epilogue: After the Madness   238

Prologue – Ambush at Kirchborchen

"American recce 800 metres!"

My stomach turned over, and a cold sweat began to overwhelm me. Marco wasn't faring much better. Max took us both by the arms and pushed us to the back of the room. "It's okay, boys. Let them get real close. They are less effective up close, trust me on this. Just relax! You know how to use your weapons, so there is no problem, agreed?" We nodded, this Russia and Normandy veteran knew how this would play out. All we had to do was our duty for Germany, and make sure every shot counted. "Stay below the window, prepare your weapons, and wait for my orders. Whatever you hear in the street, do not look out until I say so, do you understand?" With that, Max moved into the next room to calm Karl and Bruno, who were getting just as agitated as us. We dragged all our weapons and equipment to the rear of the room, and sat on the bed. Despite my trembling hands, I managed to prepare my Panzerfaust for action, and I then helped Marco with his. There were an extra two rockets each in the room, and it felt wise to prepare them also, since there was every chance of more than one target to shoot at below us. And it gave our hands something to do, other than shake. I took hold of my rifle and ensured the magazine was fitted properly, and I had easy access to my additional magazines, because what tends to accompany tanks? Infantry.

Marco and I were soon set to go. With strict orders not to look out of the window, there was really nothing else left to do than just sit on the bed, and wait for the time to fight. I sat quietly, trying to tune in with all that was going on outside. I heard the odd clatter of boots on the road, probably where some of our guys were setting up for the ambush. I could hear the constant drum of engine noise, and occasional revving some distance away, but was yet to establish which side was making the noise.

"American armour 800 metres, recce vehicles 600 metres," came the cry from somewhere downstairs. My stomach tightened all the more. Very shortly, all hell was going to let loose. I started to shiver with what could only be described as pre-match nerves. I looked at Marco. He looked just as terrified as me, and he broke into a broad grin as his eyes started to well up, tears streaking down his face. It was okay to cry. I wasn't going to ridicule him for that, and I was only just holding it in myself.

Max burst into the room, which scared the shit out of the pair of us. He slid to his knees, full of excitement. "The Americans are marching in column, not battle formation. This is just too easy." With that, he scrambled back to Bruno and Karl. Marco and I just looked at each other, and shook our heads at Max's supposedly amazing news. Max, a veteran of such scenarios, clearly had the experience to see the good in every situation; the Americans marching in column, by the sound of things it meant they were just bumbling along without a care in the world, thinking they would soon be in Paderborn, in time for coffee and doughnuts. All of a sudden, my chest filled with pride, and my fears evaporated away. They would not be in Paderborn tonight or any night, because we were going to stop them here, today!

"Recce 300 metres," came an update from below. We moved below the window on our haunches, ready to spring up for action. My hands were sweating like mad, and yet my mouth was bone dry. I cradled my Panzerfaust in my hands, running through my mind the firing drills taught just the other day on the Senne landscape. If the weapon failed and didn't fire, I would throw it at the nearest tank, in the vain hope it would launch and cause some damage. I put the Panzerfaust carefully on the floor, worried the enemy recce crew would hear it over the engine noise, which was just ridiculous, but I was so hyped up, I would hear a mouse fart in a hurricane. I wiped my slippery hands over my thighs in an attempt to dry them. They were as dry as they were going to be, and as I picked up the rocket once more, I could hear the drone of vehicles in the street, slowly creeping past, below our window.

This was it, surely. Max, give the command.

I flicked my eyes to Marco. He was breathing heavily, and blinking like he had something in both eyes. I was pretty sure above the din of engines, I could hear his heart beating, or could it have been mine? But the drone below us started to fade, since the enemy recce vehicles were being allowed through, in order for us to get the main prize, the tanks.

Heavier engines could soon be heard very close to our windows. They slowly grew louder, and the building started to vibrate. Ornaments stated to dance across their respective surfaces, some clattering to the ground. The engine noise built to a climax, the din horrendous, as what could be the first enemy tank passed under our position.

"FIRE," roared Max.

Part One: The Battle

Chapter One - The March

Never did I think that at 18 years old, I would be fighting a war on the outskirts of my own hometown.

Our mission was to destroy the Americans at Kirchborchen, six kilometres south of Paderborn. They were literally just a few kilometres away, and I would be a liar if I didn't admit I was scared. We were conducting anti-armour ambush training on the Senne, just north of Paderborn, when our instructors told us to pack up our gear to march south. The direct route to Kirchborchen was out of the question, so we were to march through Marienloh, Neuenbeken and Dahl, arriving in the early hours.

It was just as well we didn't go through the centre of Paderborn. The British bombers pounded the rail yards there, like you wouldn't believe. Their bombs were so powerful, we felt the concussion of the raid, as we began to skirt our way around the outskirts of the city. I could only pray quietly to myself that mother was okay, and Bad Lippspringe had been spared. Bad Lip lay on the northeast outskirts of the city, and I would like to think there was nothing of real value that would attract the attention of the bombers. But who knew how inaccurate their bombing was, stranger things had happened. If they came to learn of our column moving through the darkness to engage the Americans, it would not end well for us. Marching on the roads was out of the question, so we were only able to march in the drainage ditches that ran alongside; a mixture of waterlogged horseshit and mud. Slogging through the thick sludge was exhausting, the whole experience made all the more amusing and grim in equal measure, when someone in the column slipped and ended up on their knees. I made it my mission to stay on my feet, since I was not in the mood to bathe in horse crap. Small groups of tanks rumbled and grinded past our column throughout the march, flicking mud and crap all over us. The tanks were a mixed bag of our heavier and lighter beasts. Heavy Panthers with their 75mm guns intermingled with Jagdpanthers, a tank destroyer variant with a fixed turret, capable of knocking out most variants of American Sherman tank, tanks which were also used by the British and Russians. There were also a few of our 88mm-gun Tiger tanks rolling by. Our instructors had told us all about the Tiger and its reputation in Russia, the enemy losing their nerve on the battlefield, as soon as it became apparent that Tigers were in the area, a fact which buoyed my confidence in the machines, since I was sure we would see the Americans off in next to no time with the Tigers' devastating firepower.

Our Company rested briefly on the route, to allow the stragglers to catch up. The machine-gunners were not enjoying the effort, since they carried pretty much the full load; gun, tripod, sight, and as much belt-link ammunition as they could carry. The remainder didn't fare much better. We were all loaded with anything we could use to slow the Americans down.

As we trudged off the Senne towards Marienloh, we passed behind a series of trucks that were filled to the point of spill with Panzerfaust; crude yet effective rockets that could knock out a Sherman, no problems at all. The Panzerfaust was a basic thin-tube design, with a very crude sight and firing mechanism. The warhead itself was a large bulbous projectile that had enough explosive power to penetrate any vehicle the Americans could throw at us. The skill required to use the rockets was not so much in your marksmanship, it was simply having the balls and nerve to allow the tank to get real bloody close, maybe 100 hundred metres or less. Our instructors, who were now our battle commanders, constantly drummed it home that we must not panic when enemy tanks were close, experience in Russia teaching them well. Enemy tanks were less dangerous, the closer they came, since they were nothing more than a large metal box with scared people inside. Allow them to stand off at distance and exploit their weapon sights and firepower, and it would become a nightmare for any infantry trying to knock them out.

As we crossed farmland just short of coming down into Dahl, Paderborn was a bright glow over our right shoulders. The bombers had hit her hard, and continued to do so. The city centre was nothing more than an inferno, so bright it lit up the surrounding streets, and those large buildings that remained standing. I looked in the general direction of Bad Lip. It appeared to remain hidden in the darkness, which suited me just fine.

My shoulders ached with my equipment, cutting into my shoulders. But it was no use complaining. Everyone was in the same boat, including our instructors. My standard issue helmet, with its grey and green fleck helmet cover, was wedged firmly on my head; sweat slowly running down my temples, gathering under my chinstrap. My grey field tunic was hidden under my fleck smock, which was just a large, thin lightweight jacket. My grey field trousers were tucked into my leather jackboots, and in no fear of falling down, due to my braces that had the trousers wedged, right up the crack of my arse. I just couldn't be bothered to deal with it. My fighting gear consisted of my leather yoke and belt; the yoke formed a Y-shape between the shoulder blades, and went over the shoulders to help hold the weight of the gear. On my belt, I had pouches to hold my rifle magazines, a water bottle, my gas mask and canister, and my mini-shovel, which I would use to dig into my new position at Kirchborchen, if need be. As for weapons, I was sporting the STG-44, an assault rifle, which I had slung across my right side. A Panzerfaust was in my left hand, two stick grenades squeezed down the front of my leather belt. I also had the delight of carrying a tin of belt ammunition for the machine-gunners, who had to feed the hungry appetite of their MG-42s, a terrific weapon. I had used it on the ranges, and found it to be very effective.

We began to descend towards Dahl, skirting to the right on what would be the last stretch into Kirchborchen. The bombing of Paderborn all but finished, the drone of the bombers fading away. They had done what they came to do. Every now and again, you could hear muffled explosions, as fuel and other combustibles went up in flames. My mind started to wander. What had I got myself into here? I was the youngest of three boys. I was literally at the tail end of my training on the Senne, when we got orders for Kirchborchen. My eldest brother, Willi, was killed in France the previous year. Manfred, the middle sibling, had not been in touch for some time. Last I heard, he was in Russia. I hoped he was okay. I wished he would at least write to mother to put her at ease, to let her know all was well. It was no secret the Russians didn't take SS prisoners, since we were the best German soldiers on the battlefield, therefore the most dangerous.

Before long, Kirchborchen came into view, and we slowly made our way down into a broad ravine. We crossed a river via a road bridge. As we made our way up the other side, we were ushered to the left side of the road into a field, and told to rest. It was a very welcome command. I slumped against a grass bank, backing onto the road. Straightaway, the feeling in my shoulders felt like a gift from the gods. I adjusted myself so I could get to my water bottle, but it was not as easy as I had hoped. The lad in front of me on the march, Marco, leaned over to help. "Thank you, my friend," I said.

He nodded. "No problems." He had shared my barracks on the Senne, and could not have been much older than me. He was from Minden, I knew that much, but other than that, we hadn't had much to do with each other. We sat there, leaning against the bank, looking out over someone's farmland, waiting for our next move. I peered left and right along the bank. Everywhere, there was activity. Sleeping, nose-picking, ball-scratching, smoking, farting. As far as I was concerned, the SS was not known for its charm. How some of the lads ever landed a girlfriend was a mystery to me.

Word came down the line for commanders to move to the front. They struggled to their feet, but then just trudged their way up; the perks of being in charge, I suppose. I removed my helmet to get some air to my sweaty brow. A chill swept through me rather quickly as my sweaty body began to dry out, but it didn't prevent my heavy eyelids from starting to close. I would savour the brief respite, sure it would be some time before an occasion presented itself again.

After a while, our commanders came back down the line to join us. I wasn't too sure for how long I had drifted off. Max, our commander, knelt down in front of me. "Right, my lads," he called, "listen up." His lads consisted of me, Erik, and about eight others to my right and left. "We have just sighted where we will be taking up positions. The Americans made a huge land grab yesterday, since them lazy army bastards did nothing to slow them down. Lead American elements will be knocking on our door, by mid-morning tomorrow at the latest. Our job is to hit them hard, and then move back to a stone quarry, which will be our secondary position. It will give us some breathing space, as the Americans become more cautious." We all looked at each other. It suddenly dawned on us that this was going to be for real. "Hey, listen, you lot. We need to stop the Americans tomorrow. We cannot allow them Paderborn. If they take Paderborn, they then have an open road to Berlin. Do you understand?" We all nodded. "The Americans hate SS. If they capture you, but don't shoot you on the spot, they will hand you over to the Russians, and those cowboys will use your mothers and sisters as whores." My stomach turned over. "Get ready to move," he began to conclude. "As we move up to our positions, I will point out the stone quarry to you. When you hear the order to break clean, you are to make your way there with your equipment and any wounded, is that clear?"

We struggled to our feet. I adjusted myself again, making my gear somewhat more comfortable, and joined the column on the road. What came as somewhat of a surprise was the large number of civilians coming out of their houses, making their way past us towards the bridge. Old and young alike were carrying what they could stuff into a suitcase, mothers fitting whatever they could carry under their baby carriages. One old man in particular spoke rather loudly about it being left to children to hold back the Americans; the fighting men lost in Russia. One of our instructors told him to be silent and go away, but the old fool continued to babble away. I was young, let it be said, but I wasn't going to let the Americans have my hometown, not whilst I had the means to stop them. I peered down at my Panzerfaust. I had good intentions planned for it; a burning American tank, by my hand.

Chapter Two – The Master Bedroom

We began to move off up a hill. It wasn't long before those up front pointed to the right and indicated the stone quarry. I had a good long look at it, since I had every intention of seeing it again. We kept to the left side of the road. Behind us, there was commotion as a platoon of four Panthers slowly made their way across the bridge, their commanders waving civilians out of the way. Once across the bridge, the tanks pulled off the road and parked up. So by the look of things, we would have tank support when the Americans turned up; it made me feel a little better. As we began to make our way between the houses, Max told our squad to stay put, while he looked around the house assigned to us, to determine exactly where we were going to fight from. It wasn't long before he returned, and beckoned us forward. He forced open large wooden cellar doors, and we followed him down into the darkness.

We got used to the low light conditions. Max's instructions were from the school of combat, learnt in Russia. He told us the cellar was where his reserve was going to be. The house had two floors above the cellar. Machine-gunners were to occupy the ground floor, those with Panzerfaust the top floor, the riflemen acting as reserve. The method to the madness was for the Panzerfaust teams to hit the vehicles from above, which in terms of direction of your fire is a weak point on any vehicle. The machine-gunners were to deal with crews bailing out, riflemen plugging the gaps, should any of us be killed or wounded. He only wanted machine-gunners and Panzerfaust teams to occupy the road side of the house, since the plan was to knock out as many vehicles as we could in one shock attack, and then withdraw to the quarry. He didn't want his fighting power leaning out of windows, since it would just make too good a target for American tanks to ignore. The reserve would also act as stretcher bearers, getting casualties into the cellar, ready for the break-clean.

Max took me, Marco, and two other guys, Bruno and Karl, to the top floor, pairing us up. Bruno and Karl were to be put into what looked like a children's bedroom. Marco and me got the master bedroom. Both rooms looked over the main road flowing through Kirchborchen. "They will probably send their shitty little recce vehicles through first," Max surmised, "just to check the way ahead. Whatever you do, don't be seen by the recce guys, or the game is up, clear? Do not be tempted to take on the recce vehicles, the boys below you will eventually take care of them. You are to take on the tanks, nothing else. If any of their infantry get into the house, stay quiet. Only fire at them if they come into your room, understand? Remember, only fire on the tanks when I say so, not before. Hold your nerve, and give them hell."

Marco and I grinned at each other, not too sure whether it was excitement or just nerves. "The road goes out of sight, only about 50 metres away," observed Marco.

Max nodded. "Indeed it does, young Marco. You want the tanks committed to your killing area, with you not committed to theirs. You will be shooting down at them. They cannot elevate high enough to shoot at you. Remember guys, tanks only. Aim just below where the turret meets the body. As soon as the first rocket is on its way, get away from the bloody windows, or else you might not be around long enough to admire your handiwork. Prepare the next rocket at the back of the room, then quickly step forward and engage the next vehicle, okay?

"Get some rest. Stay away from the windows until I say so. I'm going to brief up the rest of the guys, and then the reserve guys are going to prepare whatever food is left in the house for us." He made his way downstairs to put the finishing touches to his plan.

I didn't take my belt kit off, but laid all my ammunition, rifle and grenades on the floor beneath the windows, along with my helmet. It would be getting light soon, and the Americans would not be too far away.

We closed the windows, and took the opportunity to lay on the bed, resting our eyes. Sleep would not come at first. Too much was going through my head. Mother, Willi, Manfred, impending combat, the war, fear of capture, fear of dying. What have you got yourself into here, Erik? The room was warm and cosy, which made me doze until my own snoring woke me up. I felt a pang of guilt, knowing that the family living here, all but a short time ago, had felt the need to flee. I detected a faint aroma of soap and perfume, and what could only be described as the smell you experience in a room where people slept. I wondered if the family and their children would have somewhere safe and warm to sleep tonight, with friends or extended family. I didn't want to be fighting in pretty much my own neighbourhood. All through my training, and even earlier in the Hitler Jugend, I had visions of slaying the Russians on the Eastern Front, far away from our women and children. The last real news we received from the front was that we were holding the Russians at bay, far from German borders, which gave us all a sense of security. Here, we had to fight just as hard to keep the British and Americans from exploiting our mothers and sisters, since should we lose, all our men folk would be handed over to the Russians as slaves. How long would it all last? Germany was a wounded animal, no two ways about it, but we couldn't allow our nation to be conquered by the Russians in the east, or the British and Americans in the west.

The clatter of tank tracks and the roar of engines made me panic, and sit bolt upright on the bed. Marco sat up, but not for long. He lost his perch, and fell to the side, causing the bedside table and lamp to crash to the ground with a clatter. I tried to get a feel for where the tank noise was coming from. I heard heavy boots on the staircase, near the top. All my weapons were on the other side of the room. Had we slept through the American advance? Was American infantry in the house?

A dark figure walked into the room. It was Max. "What are you pair of clowns doing?" Relief washed over me. Marco clambered to his feet and redressed the side table. Max sat on the end of the bed. In his hands was a piece of paper with some pencil markings. He beckoned us to gather round, having made a sketch of the town. "Here's the town. Here's us." He used a pencil as a pointer. "And here's the direction the Americans are expected to come from. The engines you can hear are those Panthers that crossed the bridge just behind us. They are split into pairs, and will be set rear, left and right of us, near the river. Their aim is to deal with any American armour or infantry movement. They are under strict instructions not to fire at any of the buildings, friendly forces are in all of them. During the battle, they will only take on infantry outside. Close combat will have to take care of any enemy getting into the houses, understand?" He noticed we had closed the windows. "Keep the windows open. I don't want any fucking around with trying to get shutters open, since that will just draw fire very quickly. So get it sorted." We opened the windows as he began to walk towards the door.

"American recce 800 metres!" came a shout from downstairs. My stomach turned over, and a cold sweat began to overwhelm me. Marco wasn't faring much better.

Max took us both by the arms and pushed us to the back of the room. "It's okay, boys. Let them get real close. They are less effective up close, trust me on this. Just relax! You know how to use your weapons, so there is no problem, agreed?" We nodded, knowing all we had to do was our duty for Germany, making sure every shot counted. "Stay below the window, prepare your weapons, and wait for my orders. Whatever you hear in the street, do not look out until I say so, do you understand?" He moved into the next room to calm Karl and Bruno. It sounded as though they were getting just as agitated as us. We dragged all our weapons and equipment to the rear of the room, and sat back on the bed. Despite my trembling hands, I managed to prepare my Panzerfaust for action, and I then helped Marco with his. There were an extra two rockets each in the room, and it felt wise to prepare them also. It gave our hands something to do, other than shake. I took hold of my rifle and ensured the magazine was fitted properly, and I had easy access to my additional magazines, knowing infantry would accompany the enemy tanks.

Marco and I were soon set to go. With strict orders not to look out of the window, there was really nothing else left to do than just sit on the bed, and wait for the time to fight. I sat quietly, still trying to tune in with all that was going on outside. I heard the odd clatter of boots on the road, probably where some of our guys were setting up for the ambush. I could still hear the constant drum of engine noise, and occasional revving some distance away, but it wasn't clear which side was making the noise.

"American armour 800 metres, recce vehicles 600 metres," came a second cry from downstairs. My stomach tightened all the more. Very shortly, all hell was going to let loose. I started to shiver with what could only be described as pre-match nerves. I looked at Marco. He looked just as terrified as me, and he broke into a broad grin as his eyes started to well up, tears streaking down his face. It was okay to cry. I wasn't going to ridicule him for that, and I was only just holding it in myself.

Max burst into the room, which scared the shit out of us. He slid to his knees, full of excitement. "The Americans are marching in column, not battle formation. This is just too easy." With that, he scrambled back to Bruno and Karl. Marco and I just looked at each other, and shook our heads at Max's supposedly amazing news. Max, a veteran of such scenarios, clearly had the experience to see the good in every situation; the Americans marching in column, by the sound of things it meant they were just bumbling along without a care in the world, thinking they would soon be in Paderborn, in time for coffee and doughnuts. All of a sudden, my chest filled with pride, and my fears evaporated away. They would not be in Paderborn tonight or any night, because we were going to stop them here, today!

"Recce 300 metres," came an update from below. We moved below the window on our haunches, ready to spring up for action. My hands were sweating like mad, and yet my mouth was bone dry. I cradled my Panzerfaust in my hands, running through my mind the firing drills taught just the other day on the Senne. If the weapon failed and didn't fire, I would throw it at the nearest tank, in the vain hope it would launch and cause some damage. I put the Panzerfaust carefully on the floor, worried the enemy recce crew would hear it over the engine noise, which was just ridiculous, but I was so hyped up, I would hear a mouse fart in a hurricane. I wiped my slippery hands over my thighs in an attempt to dry them. They were as dry as they were going to be, and as I picked up the rocket once more, I could hear the drone of vehicles in the street, slowly creeping past, below our window.

This was it, surely. Max, give the command.

I flicked my eyes to Marco. He was breathing heavily, and blinking like he had something in both eyes. I was pretty sure above the din of engines, I could hear his heart beating, or could it have been mine? But the drone below us started to fade, since the enemy recce vehicles were being allowed through, in order for us to get the main prize, the tanks.

Heavier engines could soon be heard very close to our windows. They slowly grew louder, and the building started to vibrate. Ornaments stated to dance across their respective surfaces, some clattering to the ground. The engine noise built to a climax, the din horrendous, as what could be the first enemy tank passed under our position.

"FIRE," roared Max.

I sprung up like a ferret, and before me was the most surreal scene I could ever have imagined. Beneath us was what could only be described as a traffic jam; green and brown armour crammed into a confined space on the road. We didn't need to aim, just point the rocket at the nearest solid, smelly clattering mass. I flipped the Panzerfaust onto my right shoulder and pointed at a pair of tanks left of our window. Two nearer tanks were easy prey for the team in the house to our right. I squeezed the firing lever. There was a deafening roar as my rocket streaked away, and smashed in a flurry of sparks into a target. I dropped to the floor, and scrambled to the rear of the room, going for my next rocket. Marco had fired too. He was right behind me, scrambling frantically for another rocket. I picked a rocket up, taking a second to compose myself. All the tension was gone, my mind clear of all reservation and doubt. I had been baptised into the exclusive club that is combat. As I stood to launch myself at the window once again, loud vibrating fire of an MG-42 could be heard, the bullets almost instantly causing high-pitched sounds as they struck steel. I stepped forward to the window. My original target was billowing smoke, but no flames were visible. Its crew lay sprawled over the front and side of the smouldering hulk; the boys downstairs had already dealt with them. I looked left. Undamaged tanks were trying to reverse, but tanks smouldering behind them were preventing their escape. I took care to aim at one that was trying to turn between the houses opposite. As I fired, it was engulfed in showers of sparks, smashed by several rockets at once. It stopped dead, smoke billowing from its back engine decks. It was sprayed with machinegun bullets, stopping the crew from bailing out. It looked like a huge beast that had kicked a hornets' nest. The crew never emerged.

I scrambled to the rear of the bedroom once again, cursing myself for getting caught up spectating, which could very easily have killed me. Marco stepped forward and fired his second rocket, at an armoured target, I presumed. He scampered over to me, and we took hold of our third and final rocket each. We had the taste for tank hunting.

"American infantry in the house!"

My blood ran cold instantly, as the dull thud of grenades exploding could be heard from the cellar. The concussion caused the floorboards beneath our feet to crack and creak. There was a chattering of submachine guns, screaming, shouting, more grenade thuds. Marco grabbed my arm. "Remember what Max said. Stay quiet until they come into the room." I'm glad he remembered, it seemed so long ago.

The chaos downstairs subsided. We heard different voices shouting the same thing; 'Break clean!'

We looked at each other, waiting for the familiar voice of Max. "Break clean, you fucking idiots!" he roared up the stairs, which despite the insult, made us chuckle with relief. Ensuring we had everything with us, we made our way quickly onto the landing. As I got to the top of the stairs, I was hit side-on by a solid mass, sending me crashing against the wall, and then clattering down the stairs, a greenish-grey mass on top of me. I ended up in a heap at the bottom. Winded, I tried to curse out load, but a burning sensation in my chest did nothing but produce a hacking cough.

The greenish-grey mass turned out to be Bruno, the fucking oaf! Max stood over us, shaking his head; MG-42 in one hand, rifle in the other. "Germany's finest!" he jibed, then ran out into the street. I untangled myself from Bruno, and then noticed two fleck-covered bodies, slumped in a crumpled heap below a window frame. Olive green mixed with mud could only make them Americans. Flecks of blood decorated the wall. The place reeked of cordite, and the copper tang of fresh blood; clear evidence of close combat.

The dull thud of a nearby explosion snapped me out of my trance, and we made off after Max. As far as the Americans went, it was a similar story in the street, let me tell you. Their tanks were smouldering heavily, engines still running; the heavy pungent smell of gasoline hanging in the air. Dead tank crew members hung out of their hatches. Other dead crew were in crumpled smouldering heaps on the road. Wounded lay groaning in the street, some maybe playing dead, so as not to attract gunfire. We ran mob-handed down the road towards the quarry, our heads on swivel; trying to locate our squad members, also checking for active American infantry. The quarry would be our next defence line, since I was sure the Americans would not let us get away with the ambush.

Chapter Three – Tank Assault

The enemy recce vehicles were just short of the quarry entrance; twisted smouldering wrecks, their crews slumped in sitting positions, riddled with bullets, faces smashed and caved in like eggs from the impact of various projectiles. Some dead lay by the roadside, no doubt having attempted to get away, their blood pooling beneath them, slowly trickling down the kerbside towards the bridge.

As we entered the mouth of the quarry, there was sheer calamity before me. Our wounded sat at the side of the track, being dressed in bandages by medics clucking around them. Officers and NCOs were pushing and shoving shell-shocked men into fighting positions, other officers consulting maps, pointing towards a lip of the quarry. Max guided us to a patch of ground, where he wanted us to sit tight. We put our MG-42s down at our feet. "Wait here while I find out where these clowns want us." He made his way into the melee of wounded, and those still fit to fight. Marco and I slumped against a wall, just to catch our breath. I took greedy gulps from my water bottle, nearly ending up wearing most of it. Close to the bridge, Panthers on the riverbank started firing. The Americans had to be trying to push on. Max came jogging back over. "Grab your shit. We are not staying here. The Americans will fuck us up in here. We are moving back towards the river, right now."

I scrambled to my feet and took up my MG-42, carrying it over my shoulder. To make things a bit easier for me, Marco took my rifle and Panzerfaust. I rearranged my belt of ammunition so it wasn't twisted, and I could fight quickly if need be. Max led us out of the quarry into a roadside ditch, leading down towards the bridge. Others from the quarry began to follow. Two Panthers above the quarry joined in the bombardment. As I rather quickly scampered after Max, I noticed the Panthers by the bridge rocking backwards on their sprockets and tracks, flurries of sparks as they took the punishment of the American armour. Our tanks replied in kind, which was comforting, since they were keeping the Americans busy. But as we drew near a span of the bridge, a couple of riverside Panther crews leapt out of their tanks, scrambling to join us in the ditch. "Out of fuel, can't move," said one of the grubby, sweaty, black-clad panzer crewmen.

Max leaned towards Marco, taking my rifle from him, and threw it at the crewman. "Welcome to the infantry, follow me!" The crewmen's faces were a picture, which caused Marco and me to chuckle; no more languishing in a tank, just a muddy ditch with the rest of us.

Our now large group of men scrambled down to the riverbank. The river was rather shallow, the riverbed clearly visible. Without ceremony, Max jumped in and waded across. We blundered after him, our new panzer recruits following. The water was cold, knee-deep. It poured into our boots with no effort, great.

On the far bank, we quickly emptied our boots, then made our way towards the first row of two-storey buildings and outhouses. The gardens were separated, but two-strand fences and chicken coops were dotted about the place. Chickens clucked loudly in their dwellings, as we sought to get out of the light drizzle that had begun to coat us. Some nearby troops were breaking into first-row buildings, but Max reprimanded them. "Get out of there, you fucking idiots. They will just stand off, and shoot the shit out of the bloody building. Occupy the next row." Once again, it was a lesson learned in Russia. If you occupied an outer ring of buildings, the enemy would just sit back, and let the tanks shoot you up. By occupying inner rows, tanks and infantry had to come in closer, which then put them on your terms, evening the odds. The troops sheepishly looked at each other until the penny dropped. With newfound energy, they dashed to the second row of houses, forcing their way in. We followed Max down a road, making a beeline for a house on the right-hand side. He led us around the back, and with the gentle persuasion of a hard kick, the kitchen door gave way. We occupied the house with our panzer crews, and some other guys from the quarry. "Panzerfaust men upstairs," Max ordered. "But Erik, you stay down here with me." He looked at the gathered panzer crews. "You lot sit tight in the kitchen. I will put you guys where I want you, when it all gets crazy around here, understand?" They nodded, but their expressions gave away the fact they were so out of their comfort zone. But then again, who the fuck was comfortable about the whole situation anyway?

We all went about our business. I made my way into a communal room. Remembering Max's instructions from the ambush, I placed my MG-42 below windows, which looked out onto the road. A house opposite blocked the view of the river, and a large open field that ran down from the quarry. The buildings we occupied earlier were also out of sight. I took comfort, thinking the Americans could not have a clear view of the building I was in. I opened the windows and shutters, then moved to the back of the room, sitting in a comfortable chair. I placed my helmet on my right knee, and surveyed the room. Beautifully kept, everything looked in its right place; no sign of people rushing to pack possessions, all very tidy and orderly. A large shrank unit along the left wall was adorned with lovely framed family pictures. There was evidence of children; pictures of babies and toddlers were placed all over the room. I pondered the fate of the family; total strangers to me, but I wished them good health. I felt a pang of guilt, since I would shortly bring war to their beautiful room.

I heard movement upstairs, probably Max siting guys. Boots sounded on the stairs; someone clattering down into the kitchen at the back. Max came into the communal room with one of the panzer crewmen; the guy Max had thrown my rifle at. "Young Bobby here is going to fight this position with you, okay?"

Max quickly disappeared. Bobby sat in a comfy chair next to mine. I leaned over, and offered my hand. "I'm Erik, nice to meet you, Bobby. Sorry the circumstances couldn't be more appealing."

Bobby grinned, accepting my hand. "Nice to meet you, Erik. Let's hope we can bore our grandchildren with this meeting, don't you agree?" I noticed he wasn't that young, certainly older than I. The long scar on his left cheek indicated recent action in the service of the Fuhrer, or a tough childhood. We both sat back. I felt at a loss as to what to talk about, but played it cool. He broke the ice. "Are you from around here, Erik?"

"Yeah. Bad Lippspringe, just north of Paderborn. You?"

"Frankfurt; the town on the Oder, as opposed to the big city further west."

I winced. "Any news from there?"

He looked down at his lap. "The Russians are there, that's all I know."

It was clear all was not well in the east. The Russians were in Bobby's hometown, and therefore in our homeland. Not good at all. I just hoped our guys over there could keep them from moving west. Those lazy army bastards would as usual leave it to the SS to hold the line and smash the Russians. What have you got yourself into here, Erik?

I heard the rumbling groan of what I could only guess was an armoured vehicle; the grind of transmission, the rumbling getting louder, causing the house to shudder. The ornaments danced slightly. Max came back in with his trusty piece of paper. He sat on the right arm of my chair, pencil poised. "Here's the quarry, the bridge and river, and this is how the houses sit in the street." We shuffled around to get a better view of his new sketch. "Next to us is a Jagdpanther, ready to go. We've got our guys sited in these houses; here, here, and here. At the entrance to the road, next to the bridge, there are MG-42 units that will take care of an infantry crossing. Our Jagdpanther, plus a couple of 20mm flak guns further to the right, will deal with an armoured approach." I wasn't a tactician, but it didn't sound like much to stop the Americans. "We've got a couple of guys in an observation position in the front row of houses," continued Max, "that will drip feed information to us, should the Americans move out of the quarry. When an enemy tank is hit, you spray gunfire like a bastard, and be prepared for their infantry, got it?" I nodded, but Bobby didn't seem quite as confident without his Panther. Max placed his hand on Bobby's shoulder. "You'll be fine. Just do what Erik does, and don't get killed." Great advice, if there ever was any. Bobby nodded, still not completely sold, but tough shit, it was what was happening, so he'd better step up and help me hold the house. Ever busy, Max quickly left the room.

I heard the sound of engines revving and roaring, with unmistakeable echoing in the quarry's confined space. If I was a betting man, the Americans were getting their act together, before taking another shot at the title. In my mind, I ran through what they would have to do to get into a position to blast the house into rubble. I didn't think we had enough left locally to hold them in the quarry. Once out of the quarry, they would probably just be able to see the top of our roof. But unless they reduced the outer ring house in front of us to rubble, they would have to get across the field leading down to the river to make an angle for a shot at us, meaning they would have to dance with the Jagdpanther and flak guns.

I heard commotion in the kitchen; rattling of pots and pans, running water, breaking of crockery, troops cursing. The usual calamity when you were trying to be quiet. It wasn't long before I smelt the aroma of coffee, and what could only be described as vegetables being cooked. It suddenly dawned on me that I hadn't eaten since supper last night on the Senne. Max's earlier promise of breakfast hadn't materialised because the Americans decided to turn up; how rude of them. To be honest, I wasn't fussed by what was being cooked, since I didn't have to cook it, and to top it off, I was bloody hungry.

Max leaned around the door. "Take it in turns; get in here, and get some food."

I looked at Bobby. "You go first, and I will wait."

By the time I made my way into the kitchen, it was in total disarray. Panzer crewmen had become combat cooks. They must have used every pot and pan to prepare food. Potatoes and other vegetables were in pans and pots on the kitchen table. A large jug of coffee was perched on the end. To be fair, it all smelt rather appealing. "Not your mother's quality, I'm afraid," one of the crewmen piped up, "but better than a kick in the tits." Fair point. Bobby hadn't got anything yet, so I grabbed a small pot.

One of our chefs poured me a coffee, shoving two forks into my hand. "Share with Bobby. Plenty more coffee, if you want it." Very nice.

I scampered back into the communal room, taking care not to pour the red hot coffee over my hand. Bobby pulled our two chairs together, a coffee cup in his hand. We balanced the pot and our cups on the arms of the chairs, wanting to eat in comfort. We tucked greedily into the pot with the forks, taking no prisoners, shovelling it in like pigs in a trough. Our mothers would have disapproved, let's put it that way. The food was basic, but certainly did the trick. Before long, our bellies were full. We took our time over the coffee, savouring every sip.

Tank fire, echoing not too far away, almost made me drop my cup in my lap. We carefully moved to the window and peered out. No commotion directly outside. The lads keeping watch in the house in front of us didn't appear to be concerned, so who the hell was doing the shooting?

Max leaned around the door again. "Keep low. I'm going to find out what the fuss is about." He scarpered away. The tank fire wasn't coming from the quarry, we knew that much. The noise echoed loudly from a different direction; the east. Did we have friendly forces in that direction? An ambush? Artillery? One thing was certain, the noise was bloody constant.

"Those are our tanks firing," piped up Bobby. "Eighty-eights, probably Tigers."

"How can you tell?"

"Shermans give off a dull thud, listen."

Amid the din, I strained to hear individual thuds. There were two different pitches of fire. If I was judging it right, the duller thuds weren't as frequent, so maybe the Americans weren't firing as much as us, but I wasn't exactly sure.

As the light began to wane, the echoing tank fire began to reduce to the odd shot, here and there. Max came back in. He summoned us out. Bobby and I kept a low profile until we were clear of the window, not standing up comfortably until we were in the kitchen. Marco, Karl and Bruno joined us around the table with the other panzer crewmen. Max beckoned in a few new faces from outside, introducing them as our Jagdpanther crew. The vehicle continued to idle and throb outside. Max asked for quiet, clearly what he had to tell us was important. "The Americans have tried to outflank us by moving a large tank force through Hamborn, just down the road. What they didn't bank on was our anti-tank screen, that just so happened to be sat in the wood line overlooking their route. What you heard earlier was our guys smashing them to a standstill. Another bloody nose for the Americans." The Jagdpanther crew stifled a chuckle, then shook hands. I guessed guys in their unit had been involved. "It will be dark soon," Max continued. "But don't get comfortable, since all we've done, once again, is stir the hornets' nest, and if any of you have met the Americans before all this, you know well enough they won't call it a day, just because we've given them a good hiding. So don't get cocky."

"Americans!" came a loud shout from outside. We scattered like bugs caught in torchlight, back to our fighting positions. My stomach turned over. I wasn't ready, which wasn't good for me. I didn't want to fight in the dark. Bobby and I got beneath our window frame and put our helmets on, ensuring our weapons were good to go. My palms were slippery with sweat again, but there wasn't much I could do about it, except wiping them on my thighs again. I was finally ready to go, heart pounding in my ears, but ready. I peered out of the window. The light was fading fast now, and it wouldn't be long before it was completely dark.

Over the idling engine of the Jagdpanther, I could just hear approaching vehicles. "Armour, troop carriers," a sentry shouted from the house in front of us, "and walking infantry, line abreast, 400 metres. More coming out of the quarry."

Shit, this place was going to get real busy soon. I heard the Jagdpanther engine change tempo, and begin to creep forward, causing our house to vibrate. The vehicle came to a standstill just short of the right side of our sentry house, whose occupants quickly vacated at a crouching run, making their way back to our window. Without ceremony, they clambered through, slumping on the floor in front of us. "The Jagd has got some work to do," said one of them, "there is fucking loads of them." Great, not what I wanted to hear. They clambered to their feet, and scrambled out of the room, probably looking for a new fighting position.

Max scampered in at a crouch. "Same drill as before, boys. Don't expose your position until I say. If they knew we were here, they would have smashed us with artillery by now, so keep away from the windows. Let the Jagdpanther do its stuff." Without waiting for an acknowledgement, he shot off upstairs. Bobby and I left our weapons under the window, and took refuge at the back of the room, behind the comfy chairs. The groaning and rattling of approaching engines became louder. The Americans were getting close. There was an almighty thud, and my world became nothing more than a high-pitched whine. The Jagdpanther was taking on the enemy. The whine faded, battle noise replacing it. I made out a rapid drumbeat, off to our right. The flak guns were now in the fight.

"Get ready!" roared Max. Bobby and I scrambled out from our little sanctuary, and got ourselves under the window; helmets on, weapons in hand, ready to fight. Getting my MG-42 onto the window frame would be a bit awkward, but not impossible. I saw the Jagdpanther fire again and again, round after round. The soundtrack of whining returned to my ears with a vengeance.

The sentry house suddenly burst with a muffled thud, showering the Jagdpanther in bricks, roof tiles and glass. As my hearing returned, the vehicle retreated away from the wrecked building, making our house vibrate violently. The Jagdpanther was dragging a lot of house debris. It pulled up level with us, and with a high-pitched squeal of engine and transmission noise, it turned sharply to the left. One of its turret hatches creaked open. A black-clad crewmen clambered out, quickly getting to work, clearing debris from the vehicle. I must have caught his attention. He stopped what he was doing and grinned, giving me a casual salute, before returning to debris clearance. Something off to our left caught his attention. He scrabbled up to the open hatch of the vehicle, and began screaming instructions. I was curious as to what the emergency was. I peered out to our left. A mud-smeared

Sherman was visible through a gap between houses. My world then became nothing more than a piercing scream, and a brilliant white flash.

As my vision swam back into focus, I could see Bobby lying on his side, facing me, hands on his ears, shaking his head. The high-pitched scream still rang in my ears. I propped myself up on my left side, and pushed myself back towards the wall under the window frame. The house began shuddering violently, ornaments dancing off their perches, hitting the floor with a muffled thud.

The vibration eased off to a slight rumble. I saw Max crawl into the room, and begin talking to us. I couldn't understand his dull muffle. He rolled his eyes, and grabbed me by my smock, sitting me upright. The scream in my ears began to fade, making his dialogue coherent. "The Americans have fallen back!" he bellowed. "Get your arses into the cellar. They will fuck us with artillery, make no mistake." I slowly got to my feet, helping him to get Bobby up and moving. Bobby was almost out of it. Bobby and I took our weapons to the kitchen, and were led to a door under the stairs. Max shooed us down some steps, and we arrived in a spacious cellar, which was rather bare, with the exception of a few wooden crates that contained a small amount of straw. I set Bobby down, and we got comfortable. My hearing was as good as fully back, so I jumped when Max shouted again from upstairs. "Get down into the cellar, you fucking idiots!" Chaotic clattering of footsteps accompanied boys joining us.

Marco gave me a wicked grin. "That was pretty intense. The Jagdpanther really gave the Americans what for."

Max arrived, put his weapon down, and put his hands on his hips. "Did those clowns fire next to our fucking house? I thought the whole place was about to collapse." He was referring to the Jagdpanther crew. Their barrel muzzle had indeed been right outside our window. They must have fired on the Sherman, and must have knocked it out, since we were still alive to complain about them. Max picked up his gun. "Stay down here, whilst I go and find out what is going on. If they are going to hit us with artillery, we need to just sit it out. They will be back." He climbed back up the steps. We all got comfortable. Some guys shed their gear. I chose to remain kitted up, but I did push the boat out, removing my helmet. I smelt the welcoming aroma of tobacco. Some guys gulped greedily from their water bottles. I slumped onto my side, with my head on my right bicep, in a vain attempt to rest.

I began to lightly doze. My snoring invited an occasional shove from Marco, who was also trying to sleep. Some of the guys chatted quietly. The subjects were home, the Russians, Hitler's fucking war, and anything else they wanted to get off their chests. There were no officers around, so talking was without restriction.

SS or not, we all knew it would take a miracle to change our current situation around. But if we just gave up, we risked being shot out of hand, or marched off to Siberia. The road to Berlin would be open, and that was just out of the question.

Chapter Four – War Crimes

Some of the lads started asking Bobby questions about fighting in Russia. He was rather candid with his answers, but explained how savage some of the engagements had been. Neither side took prisoners, and literally smashed each other to oblivion. He had been part of the relief force sent to help out at Stalingrad, but the weather and the Russians were so savage, the force hadn't got through. We didn't know the full story. During my time in training, I'd heard many stories about our brave fathers and brothers holding the city to the last man and bullet. Bobby informed us the Sixth Army was abandoned to freeze or starve, whichever came first. He told us about Kursk, a huge tank battle, where at one point our tanks were literally crashing into theirs, due to the dust. I took great interest in the tales, since they were far more vivid than what we had been told on the Senne.

He began to tell us about Jews and the Einsatzgruppen. "That's enough of that shit!" Max barked. I jumped out of my skin, since we hadn't heard him return.

Bobby stood up. "Just telling the boys about Russia."

"Don't be filling their heads with that nonsense," said Max, shaking his head. "I need you lot focused on the now, not war stories. Is that clear?"

We all nodded. Max motioned Bobby to sit back down and relax, then squatted down to our level. "The Americans have fallen back to the quarry. They will be back, don't you worry about that. We need guys in the wrecked house tonight, so we can give warning for another attack. I doubt we will have any artillery issues tonight, since they would have done it by now. Return to your fighting positions." We all clambered to our feet, and slowly shuffled up the cellar steps. Bobby was in front of me. Max took him by the arm. "No more stories about Russia, okay?" Bobby nodded. He and I made our way to the communal room. It was intact, but covered in dust. A lot of the small ornaments were smashed, all over the floor. The window shutters were almost closed. I carefully pushed them open; it was as good as dark now. I peered left, and could make out the dark mass of the Sherman. Its turret was missing. Flames licked around the gaping hole where the turret once sat, thick black smoke rising in a steady column from the back decks. I thought about the tank crew. Did the Jagdpanther kill them with the shell? Or did they bail out to fight another day? I wondered if the Americans reflected on events when they killed us; most probably, but I doubted we would ever find out.

Max came into the room. "You two get yourselves into the damaged house. I will send your replacements over in a couple of hours, okay?" We nodded, gathered up our kit and weapons, and slowly eased over the window frame, carefully lowering ourselves to the ground, before gingerly making our way across the road. As we approached the wrecked sentry house, the Sherman let out an almighty pop, along with a shower of sparks. The ammunition or fuel must have finally cooked off. We carefully made our way over shattered bricks and tiles, trying to make as less noise as possible. The ground floor was pretty much intact, but upstairs was just a mess. We decided to climb what was left of the stairs, to get a suitable perch from which we could watch the quarry. Bobby scaled the remains of the staircase first, before reaching down to take my MG-42 from me. I climbed with relative ease. Once on the landing, we carefully picked our way through the mess, and found a decent spot. It looked through a room which had collapsed in on itself. The remnants of the room provided us with some cover from the open field, some way beyond.

The scene in the field could only be described as carnage. Black hulks of vehicles stood smouldering, all over the place. Today, the Jagdpanther crew had really earned their pay. Some wrecks crackled and fizzed, popping occasionally as combustibles succumbed to heat and flame. It wasn't just tanks, some were troop carriers. Smaller pillars of smoke could be seen in the long grass; dead troops. I looked up at the sky. We had no roof; the dark sky appeared to be slightly overcast. It wasn't particularly warm, but we only had to sit it out for a couple of hours. We sat down, our backs against banisters. We cautiously tested them, fearing they might give way, but they seemed sturdy enough. I didn't put my machinegun in any particular firing position, I just kept it next to my right thigh, sitting cross-legged. Bobby had what was once my rifle across his thighs. At first, I was again at a loss for what to talk about, so for a little while, I just listened to the vehicles burn.

I thought I'd push my luck. "Why does Max get touchy about Russia?"

Bobby sighed, looking down at the rifle. "Can you imagine a place where you literally murder people, and none of your comrades bat an eyelid?" I shook my head. "We will pay dearly for our actions in Russia," he continued, "mark my words. My hometown is already in Russian hands. I dread what is going on, how far they will come west. I fear for my mother, my wife… my daughter." Stories of wholesale rape were not uncommon amongst the rumours we heard about our invasion of Russia. But the Russians were now in our homeland, our women for the taking.

He continued his story about the Einsatzgruppen and the Jews. Special squads of police, and thugs in German uniforms, apparently rounded up Jewish civilians and shot them; men, women, the old, the young, the pregnant, infants. No one was spared. He took a deep breath. "The Russians want revenge. They will not listen to the pleas of our people. They will have no mercy on us. We cannot guarantee the Americans or the British will take much pity on us. We are in a world of shit of our own making. We will pay dearly as a nation, I assure you of that, young Erik."

I was horrified. But the stories about our conduct had to be true. Why would he say such things, if they weren't so? No wonder Max was touchy about the subject of Russia. Was he involved? Had he witnessed atrocities? My stomach turned. We were in a bad position. Would the Americans also rape our women and girls? Would the British? The whole idea of it terrified me. What have you got yourself into here, Erik? "What should we do, Bobby?" I pushed.

He looked at me with glazed watery eyes and a half-smile. "Enjoy the war, Erik, because the peace will be terrible." Shit. We sat in silence for a while, both numbed. The flames on the knocked-out vehicles had subsided, for many just a pillar of black smoke to mark their demise. I looked up towards a lip of the quarry. The moon had broken through the cloud, which made the lip all the more prominent. I wondered what the American sentries up there were talking about. Home? Women? Beer? No doubt the Americans also wanted this madness to end. With all the technology and weapons at our disposal, the fight still boiled down to two armies, staring each other down across a muddy field. History had changed nothing in that sense.

Time passed slowly, until I heard a crunch and scrape of boots, picking their way through debris below us. I slowly got to my feet, which were partially numb, since I'd spent a lot of time cross-legged. I peered down the stairwell. As my vision improved, I could make out the profiles of Karl and Bruno. Karl gave me a thumbs up. I returned the gesture. Space was a bit tight on the landing, so Bobby and I clambered down, before they took over our duty. They hadn't been forced to choose our spot upstairs, but it did give the best view of the quarry and field.

Bobby led the way back to our undamaged house. We crunched and cracked our way along the road. He didn't lead me to our window. We entered the kitchen instead, and put our weapons on the table. He got a little oil lamp up to a soft light, illuminating the place. I needed a piss, so I stood at the back door, watering the garden, whilst he got the kettle on. I prepared the cups; coffee, with a generous helping of sugar I found in a cupboard. We sat at the table; very civilised, waiting for the kettle to boil. I looked at him. His eyes were closed. The water began to bubble. I had the million dollar question on my lips. "Did you shoot any?"

He slowly turned his head, and opened his eyes. "A long time ago, we were sat in a village in the middle of nowhere, with engine trouble. Our unit had moved on, telling us to catch up, once repairs were complete. It was a beautiful hot day, and we had nothing better to do but sunbathe, while waiting for the mechanics. I couldn't tell you who was Jewish or not, and to be perfectly honest, I didn't care. If there was a Jew who could fix my panzer in that village, I would have hired him, not shot him." I let out a giggle; soldiers' humour was never far from the surface in any story, no matter how dark. "A small column of our trucks arrived," he continued. "We thought it was the mechanics and spares. But it was full of soldiers and German Shepherd Dogs. They totally ignored us and moved straight into the buildings, dogs barking, and began turfing the families out. All the villagers were scared, dogs snapping at the children, making them cry. Our guys rounded up everyone, and led them away towards the far end of the village. About an hour later, there was a lot of rifle and machinegun fire from that direction, followed shortly by our friends and their dogs; laughing and joking, smoking cigarettes, all very happy with themselves, bastards. They mounted up in their trucks, and drove off in the direction of our units moving forward."

I looked at my hands in my lap. "I'm sorry to have asked, Bobby."

He grinned, standing up to deal with the boiling kettle. "It's okay, Erik. You are a bright kid. Just take what you hear from now on with a pinch of salt, that's all the advice I can offer you."

We savoured our very sweet coffee in silence. I didn't ask any more questions. Not because I had no more to ask. I was scared of the answers I would hear. I made my mind up; fight the Americans, just do my duty and no more. Our drinks finished, we made our way back to the communal room, and our comfy chairs. I stripped my gear off, and lowered myself slowly into my chair. It felt so nice and welcoming. In next to no time, Bobby was nudging me because of my snoring.

Chapter Five – Second Shove

"American armour in the street!"

I felt an almighty push. I opened my eyes, and as I began to focus, I saw Bobby below the window frame, waving frantically at me. "Get here, Erik. Americans in the street."

I launched myself from the chair, straight onto the floor, grabbing my weapons. The house was vibrating slightly, which indicated armour very close. It was as good as broad daylight outside. Had our positions literally been caught napping by a second American shove from the quarry?

Max crawled into the room. "They just rumbled straight down the main road, across the bridge. They've turned into our street, get ready!" Bobby and I grimaced at each other, judging when to spring up and take the tanks on. I knew I couldn't get the MG-42 onto the windowsill until the last moment; to warn the enemy too early would be suicide, but too late could get another of our positions in the street shot to pieces. I heard engines roaring. The building rumbled on its foundations, the remaining unbroken ornaments scattering across the floor.

To our left, the streaking roar of a Panzerschreck bazooka made the timing decision for me. I sprung up on my haunches. To my horror, I was looking straight into the eyes of a Sherman commander, his heavy machinegun pointing straight at me. He had me bang to rights; my MG-42 still sat on the floor. I pushed my feet backwards, allowing my frame to drop from sight, ensuring I was spread thin on the floor. The movement winded me. I waited for the world to disintegrate around me. There was a series of streaking roars and thuds. Sparks flickered through our window, all over us. A heavy hand grabbed the back of my smock. "Get the fucking gun up, now!" Bobby roared. I quickly got to my knees, and clumsily got the gun up onto the window frame. The Sherman was still there, dark smoke billowing from every hatch, and its engine decks. The American was slumped over his machinegun, minus his head. His blood was smeared like a young child's painting, around the machinegun mounting. His body flinched with bullet strikes, as those above us took no chances that the crew might bail out. The smoke made searching for enemy infantry difficult, since the tank took up most of our field of view. I quickly swivelled the MG-42 left and right, in a desperate search for targets.

There was an almighty snap above my head as the window frame splintered. Splinters from the shrank unit to my right began to burst across the room. Bobby dropped like a deadweight, grabbing my smock, my face smashing into the gun as he pulled me down. "Incoming," he screamed. He hunkered down as small as possible. I copied him as the world splintered around us; timber, glass, plaster, brickwork, even our beloved chairs disintegrating in front of my eyes, the Americans giving our position some considerable attention. It was relentless, heavy gunfire from desperate men. Amid the din, Max came crawling into the room, getting covered in splinters and fabric fragments. He got close enough to be heard. "Get that gun into the fucking fight, or I will kill you myself!"

I feared the Americans more than Max, but his piercing glare soon won me over. The splintering became less frequent, so Bobby and I composed ourselves for an almost certain suicidal commitment to our window. The bipod legs of my gun were still hanging on the window ledge. I just needed to lift the gun onto my right shoulder and fire. I took a deep breath and forced myself up, swinging the gun left.

Now and again, the smouldering tank smoke allowed us to see other burning vehicles. To the right, I could make out muddy, olive-drab shapes, dashing into the buildings opposite. I fired a long burst, tracer splashing all over the front of a house, flicking skywards. Every time I saw what I felt to be enemy tank crews, I hosed the general area. Due to the smoke, I couldn't confirm the results of my marksmanship. But it felt good to throw something back at them, after what they had thrown at us for the last couple of minutes. The incoming gunfire from our left began to subside. The thud of grenades began. I didn't have a clue who was using them, but judging by the concussion, they were being used indoors. I kept searching for the building I'd been shooting at. I couldn't see any movement. As my adrenaline began to fade, a throbbing in my nose and top lip became a distraction. I'd pretty much taken a face-full of the bloody gun as Bobby pulled me down. I licked my top lip gingerly; the copper tang of blood unmistakable. My nose felt like it was bloody huge. Keeping my eyes on my target house, I pouted. "How's my lip?"

Bobby didn't really give it a glance. "Your good looks won't suffer too badly, boy."

Max scrambled to the door, kneeling as he faced us. "Good work, guys. We are going across there. Once we start to move, do not, I repeat, do not fire to the right of that tank in front of you. Understand?" We nodded. He leaned out of the room, and bellowed up the stairs for those above us to move to the kitchen. Boot scuffs and clattering followed, undoubtedly Marco, Bruno and Karl. Max called Bobby to him. I couldn't make out what they were saying, so I returned my eyes to my target building.

After a few minutes of activity in the kitchen, Bobby crawled back to join me. "Max and the other guys are going to assault the house in front of us. Enemy tank crews are holding out in some of the buildings, so we are going to counterattack them, to dislodge them from the street." From our current position, we couldn't support Max's group, since the tank blocked our view. Bobby read the expression on my face. "I know, Erik. Just deal with the house you've been shooting up, okay?" I refocused on my target house, totally bewildered. Why couldn't we reposition ourselves? Maybe moving to a better vantage point would give away Max's intentions. There was a clatter of jackboots on cobbles. Max and his assault team were sprinting across the road, out of sight of us. I heard commotion; the sudden thud of grenades, followed by a piercing scream. Gunfire echoed, more grenades. Movement began in my target building. Dark shapes bobbed behind the windows on the ground floor, and behind some of the small cellar windows beneath. Some dark shapes started to fire, in what must be the direction of the house Max and his group were assaulting; dull muzzle flashes from way back in the dark rooms. I fired short bursts at the flashes. My tracer splashed through and around the windows. Before long, it wasn't just my bullets striking the brickwork around them. Max's group were assaulting my target house. I kept my bursts short and controlled, fearing Max and his guys would suddenly appear to the right of the tank, and run straight into my fire. It wasn't long before I made out Max's profile, appearing from behind the tank. I switched to potential targets on the left. Max prepared a grenade, but as he went to throw it, he slumped to the ground in a burst of red mist. His own grenade shattered his limp frame. I hammered all the windows I could see with everything I had. My ammunition belt was as good as expended when I stopped firing. I looked at Max's body, then at Bobby. He put a hand on my shoulder. "It was his time, Erik," he murmured. "His war is over." He was right, of course he was. But of all the people I thought would get through this awful mess, my money would have been on Max. He had fought his way through Russia and Normandy, and had managed to pass on his knowledge to us, as an instructor on the Senne. But he was now just a shattered bloody heap on a road in Kirchborchen. I'd never found out where he came from, or if he had any family; snippets of information you feel can always wait for another day. It was times like this that showed you how fragile life was, certainly in these situations.

The popping and fizzing sparks from the tank snapped me out of it. "Get away from the window," screamed Booby, "things inside that tank are cooking off!" He took me by the arm, and pulled me back to the remains of our comfy chairs. They were in a bad way, but anything was better than sitting on the floor, amongst the smashed remains of the room. I slumped into my chair, and had a grim scene to watch on top of the tank. The headless American became engulfed in large licking flames. As he blackened, ammunition cracked off inside the turret, causing him to flinch, slumping over his heavy machinegun. My immediate concern was the belt of ammunition still fitted to his gun, which was still pointing at us. I told Bobby. "Good point, Erik, let's get in the kitchen."

We very quickly gathered up our weapons and equipment, and scurried to the kitchen. The other panzer crewmen were gathered, drinking coffee. Numbers were rather depleted; it was basically just me and the panzer crews. Bobby poured us both a coffee. "How we doing for ammo?" he asked them.

"Couple of magazines per man," one of them piped up, "couple of grenades between us, no more Panzerfaust."

Bobby grabbed hold of the very short belt of ammo left on my machinegun. "Is this the last of it?" I nodded. "This isn't going to get us very far," he said, looking back at the panzer guys. "Let's see if there is anything of use upstairs."

We all made our way upstairs. Two fairly large rooms overlooked the street. The right-hand room was clearly meant for children; toys and trinkets on various wooden units, a small bed at either end. The room was coated in dust, with numerous bullet strikes in the high side of the right wall. The wooden shutters were badly smashed, hanging from their fittings. Large chunks of brickwork and masonry were missing from the street-side wall, scattered all over the room, glass everywhere. Whoever had to fight from the room received some serious incoming. Outside the window, a heavy light-grey smoke drifted up from the tank, causing the building opposite to shimmer. The odd flame from the tank flicked up to the windowsill. The headless American must have been reduced to a funeral pyre; a heavy scent of cooked meat hanging heavily in the air. I didn't want to look down at him, so I kept back from the window. And besides, some trigger-happy American might just be waiting to take a shot. Movement caught my eye in the house opposite. I crouched, fearing the movement to be American, but I quickly recognised Bruno's profile. He was looking straight at me, waving frantically. I gave him a thumbs up, which he returned. All appeared well with him. "Bobby," I said, "we've got friendlies in the house opposite."

"How many?"

"I don't know. I don't want to shout, and draw attention."
Bobby nodded. We didn't know what the Americans had in store for us, and we needed any German survivors with us. "Follow me," asked Bobby, "we need our people over here."

I followed him downstairs, and out the back of the house. We skirted around the right side, stopping short of the corner, the front of the Sherman just about level with us. He gestured for me to stay put, then continued forward, crouching in front of the Sherman. Peering around the side of the tank, he waved across the road and gave a thumbs up.

There was a rapid clatter of boots on cobbles. Bruno and Karl scampered past Bobby, as red tracer snapped off the cobbles, causing little stones to flick up, heading for the house to our right. As Karl and Bruno joined me, Bobby jumped back, lost his footing, and landed on his arse. He quickly turned and scrambled back to us, letting out a nervous giggle. "That was fucking close." He took hold of their smocks. "You guys okay?"

They both nodded. "Marco is dead," Bruno said. "They took his head off, as we got in through a ground floor window. Max dealt with them fuckers."

He was talking about our leader; now just another dead soldier in the middle of the street.

Chapter Six – Retreat to Paderborn

Bobby led us back to the kitchen, then back upstairs. The only ammunition we had was whatever was left around the house, and on our bodies. It was late morning, and with any luck we would get fresh troops and ammo pretty soon. Down the street to our left, towards the bridge, the odd thud of a grenade, or a burst of gunfire, broke the silence every now and again. The only constant noise was the cracking and popping of the Sherman below our window.

I was on my own in the children's room. Taking caution, I tried to peer out, to see if there was any movement in the houses opposite. I couldn't help but look at Max. Still lying there in full view. Such a shame. There were dead Americans in the street as well, but it didn't really register. They appeared as muddy green piles of rags with helmets, but Max look like a bloodied drunken soldier, asleep where he fell.

The day continued with little movement or action. It was the end of March, and therefore wasn't particularly warm. I decided to use the children's bedclothes to drape over my shoulders, to take the cold edge off. Before long, the light outside started to fade again. Bobby moved about the house, doing his rounds, seeing we were all okay. I found it rather bizarre. A few hours ago, he was bailing out of his panzer, quickly drafted into the infantry. Now he was our squad leader. I suppose that's war for you.

He peered into the room. "I'm going to try and find out what we are going to be doing tonight. Don't waste anymore ammo or grenades, unless you can hit what you are shooting at, okay?"

"Sure," I said, nodding, "could you try and scrounge some ammo for this?" I gave the MG-42 a light kick.

"I will try. I will be back as soon as I can." He made his way downstairs. I didn't want to sit on my own any longer, so I gathered up the gun and my equipment, and joined Bruno and Karl in the adjoining room. I found them sitting on the master bed, Bruno perched on the end, keeping watch out the window. Karl sat up dozing against the head of the bed, with the bedclothes wrapped around him. I sat next to Bruno. "Are you guys okay? Pretty intense, eh?"

He gave me a tight-lipped smile, his eyes glazed, probably through emotion and exhaustion. "Hopefully, we will get some more guys and ammunition shortly. I don't think we have the muscle right now to fend off the Americans again." I agreed with him. SS or not, ammo and manpower was always a factor, since without either, we were going to get overrun, sooner or later. I didn't have much to talk about, and I didn't want to know how Marco got killed. What still played on my mind was what Bobby told me; our exploits in the name of the Fuhrer and the Fatherland. I had chosen not to repeat it, unsure of anyone's loyalties or political awareness. Such gossip around the wrong people could have you in a whole heap of trouble.

It was almost dark when I heard movement downstairs, followed by Bobby's familiar voice. "Guys, grab all your gear, and get down here." Bruno gave Karl a shove, who slowly emerged from the bedclothes, gathering up his fighting gear. We trudged downstairs and met the panzer crews in the kitchen. They passed around a few cups of coffee. Bobby called for quiet. "Gentlemen, we are withdrawing back into Paderborn. We will establish a new defence line between Kirchborchen and Paderborn. I've just been talking to the Hauptsturmfuhrer a few houses down, and he has made the decision for us to move there, due to lack of manpower and ammunition. He is confident we have slowed the Americans down to a more cautious pace, and now is the right time to break from this engagement." We looked at each other, some of us nodding.

We gathered up our gear and weapons, and followed Bobby into the back garden. It wasn't very big. A high sloping, almost sheer rock ledge lay behind the gardens in the row. Off to our right in the half-light, I saw friendly troops, slowly making their way along the base of the ledge, some carrying wounded. The unwounded appeared to be in reasonable shape, although overall, the shuffling column looked a bit battered, tired and broken. At the head of the column was a rather well-built SS officer, the Hauptsturmfuhrer. He turned, gesturing for the column to stop and rest. His group was a mixed bag of SS infantry, black-clad panzer crewmen minus their panzers, and a few random troops thrown in. He approached us. I decided to keep my mouth shut. "Oberscharfuhrer," he said to Bobby, "we will leave here quietly, and make our way towards the north end of town. We will link up with reserves and armour. We can then get our wounded seen to, and the remainder of us fed and watered. With a bit of luck, we'll get more ammunition."

"Yes, Hauptsturmfuhrer."

"I will take the lead," continued the Hauptsturmfuhrer, "could you please bring up the rear. I don't want any of our wounded being left for the Americans. Thank you." He turned to his column, waving them forward. They slowly clambered to their feet; the wounded groaning, helpers hushing them. He slowly began to lead them away. We clambered up from the garden, joining the rear of the column. Hopefully, we would be well clear, by the time the Americans realised we had withdrawn. No doubt, we would soon enough have the pleasure of their company, but for now, I was confident we had smashed them to a standstill.

Progress on the retreat was painfully slow. The column stopped many times, men taking it in turns to carry makeshift stretchers, which were made from old doors, or whatever was strong and rigid enough to do the job. Some of the wounded looked in a real bad way. I don't think there was a single medic in the column, so there was no pain relief to be had, but most stifled moans and groans. If I was wounded, I would bite my lip tight, no matter how much pain I was in. I would not want to be left for the Americans. I didn't imagine they would give a wounded SS soldier anything, apart from a bullet to the head.

As we made our way out of Kirchborchen, we stopped now and again, listening to make sure only our Jagdpanther was following, the occasional sound of the tank destroyer reassuring, even if it might soon be required elsewhere. We also heard ammunition cooking off in Kirchborchen, the sound ever more distant as we progressed.

We began to encounter small groups of friendly forces. They had nothing but what they stood up in, and whatever ammunition and weapons they carried. It was a good job they had no itchy trigger fingers, since it was very dark, and things could go wrong very quickly. Every time our column met friendly forces, the Hauptsturmfuhrer had a chat with them before moving on.

The column began to stop more frequently, stretcher bearers tiring quicker. Bobby gave us a nod to take a turn, the bearers we relieved holding our weapons. The route was bloody hard work, the Hauptsturmfuhrer leading us through a maze of houses and gardens. It seemed to make the whole ordeal longer. I felt exposed without my weapon, just two stick grenades stuffed into my belt. I really started to sweat, feeling it trickle down my temples, and along the inside of my chinstrap. There was still a marching rhythm, many new stretcher bearers assuming duties, without the column even stopping.

The ground started to level out, as we entered the outer limits of Paderborn. Kirchborchen had pretty much got away from the bombers unscathed, but Paderborn was smashed like you wouldn't believe. Marching became more difficult because of the bomb damage; we had to take care we didn't slip on the loose surface of brick, timber and other fragments, or trip over exposed pipework from sewers. The scent of human shit was present, many sewers shattered. I was carrying a stretcher with Bruno, when he lost his footing and crumpled to the ground. Our wounded comrade gasped, but to his credit, made no more of a fuss. Bruno apologised and got himself together.

The road became barely recognisable, between the shattered buildings. Up ahead, I noticed a black-clad, dusty panzer crewman, clambering all over a large pile of bricks and masonry. As we drew closer, it became clear that a tank barrel was sticking out. Another crewman gave me a casual salute, identical to the one I received in Kirchborchen. We were reunited with our Jagdpanther, the crew having taken time to camouflage it amongst ruins.

We trudged on past it, the Hauptsturmfuhrer calling for a breather, 300 metres later. Bruno and I carefully placed our wounded man down. I took the weight off my feet, and had a drink. The remaining water in my bottle was just enough to take the edge off my thirst. Hopefully, I would get a chance to refill it soon. I peeled my helmet off, a cool breeze sweeping over my head. My hair was quite long on top, but I had kept the sides cropped short. It was all matted with sweat, but after running my fingers through it a few times, it felt somewhat more comfortable. The Hauptsturmfuhrer came walking down the line, stating we were to get the wounded to a halftrack, sitting a little further up the road. We gathered ourselves quickly, everyone soon loading their wounded to the vehicle, stripping them of any weapons and ammunition. The halftrack crunched over debris, as it gunned away from houses scattered in its path.

The Hauptsturmfuhrer took us back to the rest site, before we branched off left, taking up fighting positions amongst the rubble. The rubble meant our field of view was once again not great, but in the low pre-dawn light, we saw the exhaust and back decks of the Jagdpanther, 200 meters in front of us, its front and sides still coated in the remains of someone's home. The battered and bruised column were strung out in a line of sorts, the Hauptsturmfuhrer and Bobby positioned rear-centre. They were deep in conversation, only evidenced by various nods and shaking of heads. Bobby got to his feet, moving to the right-hand end of the line, gathering another panzer crewman in the process. They walked away out of sight, down the road to Paderborn, as dawn fast approached. I took the opportunity to try and get comfortable and rest. I was completely shattered, but sleep did not come easily; too many things going through my head. As I slowly began to relax, the cold started to creep in. We no longer had the luxury of a roof over our heads, the clear daybreak bringing a chilled air. Every now and again, I drifted off, only to wake with a violent shiver. I had only the clothing I was wearing, and I regretted not bringing bedclothes with me. We had pretty much passed the point of looking mean and fearsome. I just wanted to keep warm. I propped myself up on one elbow, and saw that some of the guys had a cigarette on the go. I wasn't a smoker, but I had to admit, it did give an illusion of warmth. Away in the far distance, the sound of tank fire, and the chatter of machineguns began. I wasn't overly concerned. Some other poor souls were clearly fighting for their lives, trying to keep the Americans at bay. All was quiet here. For now.

Slowly but surely, the light around us began to give away more detail. I looked at the Jagdpanther and sat up. To its right, across the road, was one of our flak guns. The light now revealed the subtle profile of its crew, crowded around the odd glow of a cigarette. Movement elsewhere caught my attention. Level with us, on the other side of the road, was a squad of infantry. About ten of them altogether, and judging by their appearance and equipment, they could well have been SS. Most were wounded in one way or another; bandages featuring heavily, blood clearly soaking through some of them. There was no sign of Bobby, who had been gone some time now. I didn't know what type of errand the Hauptsturmfuhrer had sent him on; hopefully to find us some ammunition. Up ahead, I noticed movement on the engine decks of the Jagdpanther. One of its crew was hunched over the top of the vehicle, holding binoculars. The rest of the crew were asleep behind the vehicle. "Tanks and infantry from the direction of the quarry!" he hollered. Here we go again. The Hauptsturmfuhrer scrambled down our line at a half crouch, giving those who were dozing a rough shove. Like automatons, we checked our weapons, laying our grenades out, ready for action. My MG-42 only had ten rounds on its ammunition belt, and I had my two grenades. It was not good, unless Bobby came back real soon with ammunition; real trouble was imminent.

There was a crunching of masonry behind us, and loud cursing. Bobby and his crewman dragged a large, flat wooden crate to me. They slumped in a sweaty heap, exhausted. "Erik," Bobby managed between gasps of breath, "find me a cigarette!" I scrambled up the line to his other panzer crewmen. They anticipated my arrival, producing a rather dog-eared cigarette, and a badly creased book of matches. I thanked them, and made my way back. The Hauptsturmfuhrer stood over Bobby, a grenade in each hand. He threw them roughly back into the crate. "Are they fucking serious?" he hissed. "We've got tanks and infantry approaching us, and them fat lazy bastards back there give us just a box of fucking potato mashers!" 'Potato mashers' referred to the shape of the grenades; the explosive core at one end, mounted on a thick wooden stem.

"Apologies, Hauptsturmfuhrer," Bobby murmured, crestfallen. "That's all they would give us."

The Hauptsturmfuhrer knelt down. "It's not your fault, Oberscharfuhrer. It just angers me, when the idiots sipping cognac back there expect us to hold the Americans at bay with just a box of grenades."

I gave Bobby his cigarette. He grinned, then gave the crate a kick. "Thank you, Erik. Could you dish out these to all the lads in our line."

"Sure." I didn't try to drag the heavy crate over the rubble. I grabbed cluster after cluster of grenades, gradually working my way down the line. I was a sweaty, smelly mess, when the grenades were all distributed. My group had three or four each. Not much to stop tanks, but that's all we had. I settled back into my fighting position, awaiting the inevitable. It wasn't too far away. A streaking roar of Panzerfaust from distant Kirchborchen announced the arrival there of more Americans. Muffled thuds of rockets were followed by the chattering of MG-42s, an unmistakeable sound. The soundtrack suddenly changed to the overwhelming thunder of tank fire. The Americans had raised their game, by the sound of things. We sat amongst the rubble, listening to the streak of our rockets responding to the roaring tank guns. The Americans were probably pulverising the friendly forces we passed through in the night. I wondered how on Earth our guys could extract themselves from the carnage, if at all. The tank fire sometimes ceased temporarily, silence soon filled by the muffled thud of grenades; American infantry in the houses. We could just about hear rifle fire, perhaps even the odd faint scream and shout. It all sounded rather horrendous, continuing on for some time.

Eventually, Kirchborchen succumbed to silence, although I thought I heard some yelling in an unfamiliar language. The Americans had clearly not been run out of town today. Engine noise began from Kirchborchen. There was more streaking of rockets, more tank fire.

Up ahead of us, the Jagdpanther crew scrambled into their vehicle. Here we go. The flak gun crew were moving, getting ready for action. My stomach tightened and turned over. In my short military career, I could safely say I'd had my fair share of combat, but I doubt you ever fight off the nerves. I slipped my helmet on. I looked around; everyone else was ready to go. The Hauptsturmfuhrer scampered up and down the line, giving us all a friendly pat on the shoulder, and thumbs up.

The Jagdpanther's gun thudded. The vehicle rocked back on its suspension, bricks and masonry falling from its sides. It fired again, more camouflage crumbling away. But then it violently rocked back in a flurry of sparks, building fragments flying off. The Americans had it in their long-range sights. In quick succession, it was struck numerous times, more sparks flying off its thick armour, the remaining house debris splintering away, some of it in the direction of the flak gun crew. The Jagdpanther rocked back on its suspension again, taking all the Americans could throw at it. But then black smoke began to creep out of its engine decks. Dusty black-clad crewmen scrambled out, rolling away before scampering to our line, surrounding my position. They were sweating and breathing heavily. The Hauptsturmfuhrer crawled over, to check they were okay. The Jagdpanther commander nodded. "Yes, Hauptsturmfuhrer. It would have been a damn sight better, if we had some fucking ammunition and fuel. We couldn't move, hence the camouflage." They were all armed with MP40 submachine guns, and began scrambling furiously to build up the fighting positions with bricks, timber, anything that gave half a chance of protection. The smoke pouring out of the Jagdpanther became thicker and blacker, flames licking out of the engine decks. We watched flames overwhelm the vehicle and her fittings.

The flak gun burst into life with a rapid thumping drumbeat, its crew members feeding it with large clips of ammunition. The SS infantry opposite sprung to life, dashing to the burning Jagdpanther, crawling behind it, before lining up amongst a pile of rubble. They started throwing grenades. After a series of loud echoing thuds, they stood up together. They fired their weapons, before charging out of sight, behind the rubble pile. Their rifle and submachine gun fire reported, with heavy rapid fire from the flak gun. The SS squad had clearly taken it upon themselves to face the enemy head on; remarkable, but potentially suicidal.

The flak gun started really going for it. We could only guess the targets. Small objects flew at the flak gun crew, from the rubble pile. It became horrifyingly clear what the objects were, when the crew were obscured in a dust cloud of brick and masonry. As the dust drifted off, the gun stood silent, the crew nowhere to be seen. 'Infantry!' screamed some of the guys to my right.

I focused on the burning Jagdpanther. I couldn't see any targets, but some guys started firing in that direction, their rounds splashing all over the stricken vehicle and the rubble surrounding it, causing dust to flick up, tracer screaming off in all directions. "Slightly left of the tank!" someone roared. I adjusted my gaze, and sure as shit, I saw what could have been the mud-smeared, olive-drab domes of American helmets. Everyone except me started firing, their rounds splashing all around the domes. Some guys further up towards the Jagdpanther started hurling grenades, but it was too far away, so the grenades fell short. I prayed grenade splinters found their targets, but couldn't really tell. More mud-smeared domes began to bob around the rubble pile.

"Follow me and hurl your grenades," the Hauptsturmfuhrer roared. "Then we withdraw! Move now!"

We raced forward and threw our grenades, as far and as fast as we could. Bullets snapped over our heads, smashing into our previous position. Rounds screamed off everywhere, as they clipped masonry. The enemy fire was really intense. I hunched down in some cover. Grenades burst all around the rubble pile at the Jagdpanther, dust and brick splinters flying up. The Hauptsturmfuhrer moved close to me, firing away at the enemy. Rounds were still smashing all over the place, yet there he stood, in full view of the Americans, pouring it back at them. I felt it was only a matter of time before their aim got good, and his luck got bad. Even the audible clunk of his empty magazine didn't faze him; he merely looked left and right. Then he sprinted off to one side, guys beginning to follow him. I didn't need any prompting. I scrambled out of my cover, and pushed as hard as I could through loose house debris. The snapping of rounds was very loud in my ears, as the Americans tried to cut us down in our mad dash out of there. I crested a heap of debris, and saw our lads strung out. The Hauptsturmfuhrer changed direction, back towards where the halftrack had picked up wounded.

I saw a halftrack behind a shattered house to my right. The Hauptsturmfuhrer ran to the halftrack, saying something to its crew, who were uncoupling a broken-down second halftrack. My lungs were burning as I rushed towards the vehicles. I didn't want to look back, fearing American troops were close behind, picking us off as we sprinted. My ankle turned in debris, which made me wince, but I couldn't afford to slow down. I reached the rear of one of the halftracks. The Hauptsturmfuhrer was already helping guys get inside it.

When it came to my turn to climb in, he gripped my smock, a look of rage on his face. "Where the fuck is the machinegun, soldier?" I was stunned, totally stunned. I had abandoned my weapon to the enemy. I had really fucked up. I didn't know what to say, I couldn't think straight. What possessed me to leave the MG-42 behind?

He released my smock, and began to run in the direction of the Americans. On the halftrack, Bobby stood up. "What the hell is he doing?" I asked, still not able to find words to explain my crime. The Hauptsturmfuhrer scrambled up over some rubble. As he crested the mound, the sheer volume of gunfire against him was almost overwhelming, like the world was ending. As he descended out of sight, I wondered if he had gone to his death. What have you got yourself into here, Erik?

But he reappeared on the crest of the mound, scrambling towards us with my MG-42 in his hands. He jogged up to me, stuffing the machinegun into my chest, winding me. "Don't ever do that again," he told me, glaring. "Do you understand, soldier?"

"Yes, Hauptsturmfuhrer." It was all I could muster. I couldn't believe he had survived retrieving my gun. He looked around at the other guys. "Let's get the fuck out of here." He walked around to the cab, as I quickly heaved myself into the vehicle. I doubted he would feel guilty about leaving me behind. The halftrack lurched forward, and we shot down a road.

Chapter Seven – Retreat to Schlangen

The halftrack lurched, creaked and rattled through the shattered streets of Paderborn. The bombing, two nights previous, had really taken it out of the city. As we slowly ground through the maze of streets, I was amazed how the local residents were working hard without any real direction, clearing the roads of rubble and debris. We could clearly identify the road ahead. Off to the sides, there were neat piles of bricks and other materials that remained intact, and maybe could be used in an eventual rebuild. Military traffic was light and orderly. Military police were manning the main intersections, directing troops and vehicles through the destruction. The civilians paid no attention to us. They had more pressing issues, such as recovering what they held dear from their smashed houses. I couldn't see any dead bodies on the roadsides. Maybe that terrible chore had already been dealt with the day before, whilst we dealt with the Americans in Kirchborchen.

I caught Bobby's gaze. He give me a nod and a wink. He looked tired. In fact, we were all pretty tired, my brain exhausted. It had been a while since we had anything real decent to eat. My last proper meal had been on the Senne, before the march to Kirchborchen. Some of the other guys packed in with us were dozing, but you couldn't beat a good night's sleep in a real bed. When we would see a bed again was anyone's guess; the

Americans were too close, to rest our heads on a pillow. I closed my eyes, bumping and rolling with the motion of the halftrack.

I wasn't too sure how long I had dozed, but a rough shove brought me round with a start. As I focused on the guys around me, I noticed the Hauptsturmfuhrer leaning back towards us. "We are trading space for time," he shouted over the rattling din of engine and tank tracks. "We are moving north to Schlangen, just the other side of Bad Lip. We plan to meet up with reinforcements; fragmented units, plus panzers from the north. Which such few numbers, Paderborn is now untenable to us. We are putting in a defence line at Schlangen, so we can contain the Americans here, understand?" We all just nodded at him. He eyed us suspiciously, probably not entirely convinced we had understood. I liked his explanation of the plan, though; plain, simple, and easy to remember. I just wanted us to be far enough away from Bad Lip when the shooting started, since mother was still at home. As far as I was concerned, Bad Lip held nothing of value to the Americans. I was sure Paderborn was the prize.

As we headed north towards Marienloh, the going got better, since we were clear of the damage caused by the bombers. Our pace was still slow, though, due to the sheer volume of people traffic on the road. Soldiers were marching in groups of various sizes. Women, children and the elderly had all they could carry, some of it crammed into baby carriages. More often than not, soldiers were waving the civilians out of the way of military traffic, but the civilians usually ignored them. I was concerned the civilians were moving towards our next defensive position. I hoped they would just keep walking until they had passed it.

The crowds eventually thinned out, and we speeded up somewhat. It wasn't long before we entered Bad Lip. I was suddenly overwhelmed by homesickness. There I was, dirty and tired, sat in the back of a halftrack, trundling through my neighbourhood, my home and mother merely a few streets away; truly bizarre. We lurched to a halt, people traffic again causing the hold-up. I had a revelation. I could just jump out of this bloody machine, sprint my heart out down the alleyways and vanish. The guys wouldn't know what was happening, until it was over. I could do it, no problem. But the fearful dread of reprisal overwhelmed me. What if I was followed, or the military police were told where I lived? Punishment would be swift and ruthless. Mother might be punished for hiding a deserter. They would not take pity on her, for hiding her boy from the war. I couldn't risk her being dragged into my error of judgement, so I chose to stay put in the halftrack. We lurched forward again, beginning to creep our way through the people-flooded streets.

We very slowly cleared Bad Lip, which despite my feeling of self-pity, was a good move. I'm glad our masters didn't want to make a stand there. We pushed north, our speed still dictated by civilians fleeing the fighting.

But the roads soon cleared again. We were just south of the village of Schlangen, when the sound of a small aircraft caught my attention. The sky was overcast, but the cloud base was quite high. I could clearly see a small single-prop aircraft, buzzing off to our right. It was the first aircraft I had seen for some time, but too far away to tell who it belonged to. It drifted closer to the line of the road. It was clearly not a bomber or fighter. I gave it no more of my time, and took interest in the state of my unpolished, badly scuffed boots. I would be reprimanded for such turnout, if we were still on the Senne under instruction. Our instructors would have come down on us harshly, for such cases of poor discipline. But given the circumstances now, I don't think anyone was going to lose much sleep over the state of my boots.

We rattled and squealed our way through Schlangen, just beyond the northern end. Apart from a few isolated buildings and fenced fields, we were back out on open farmland. We passed an intersection. Close by, friendly troops milled about. A couple of panzers were sited, facing back towards the village. In the other direction, the road ran off toward the Teutoburger Wald. The road was raised, dirt banks leading down on either side. The panzers were wedged into one of the banks, their crews applying turf to the front and sides of the tanks, leaving the turrets poking over the top.

The halftrack lurched off to the left side of the road, and bumped uncomfortably out into a field. We went round behind the panzers, ending up facing Schlangen. The Hauptsturmfuhrer let off an almighty stretch, scratched his arse, and clambered off the vehicle, reappearing at the rear. "Sit tight, whilst I find us a spot to set up. We should expect reinforcements from the north, anytime soon. The Americans will take their time, picking their way through Paderborn. By the time they realise there is no one to fight, our reinforcements should be here. We can then go back into town, and give them what for." He set off across the field. The guys began to come to life, slowly dragging their tired frames from the halftrack. They stretched their legs, allowing the circulation in their numb arses and legs to get flowing again. It wasn't long before we heard a wolf whistle. We turned to see the Hauptsturmfuhrer waving, beckoning us over. The position he chose was 100 metres from the two panzers. He called the halftrack forward, siting it on the bank, our centre of mass. He split the group into pairs, siting us along the bank in support. Bobby was my partner. The halftrack gunner had a mounted MG-42 with ammunition in a small turret. The driver became an infantryman, dug into the bank with our group.

We camouflaged the vehicle as best we could, leaving the turret free to traverse. Once we had finished preparing our battle positions, I was a sweat-soaked mess. I didn't smell too great; my belt kit had that pungent aroma of soaked leather. It would stiffen as it dried, which would make it a real pain to get on and off. I took my helmet off, and rested against the bank. As I ran my fingers through my sweaty matt of hair, I once again noticed the little aircraft. It was quite a welcome sight; very different to chaos, death and sorrow. It gave me a sense of carefree abandon, just gliding about at its leisure, without a care in the world. I wasn't too sure of its purpose in the area, but didn't really care.

A steady stream of civilians began passing through our position. Were they fleeing the fighting? The supposed raping? The murdering American hordes? I settled down on the bank. The little I knew about the Americans didn't point to brutality against civilians. I knew of Hollywood and the movie stars. There had been a quietly murmured admiration for American logistics and firepower, which some of our instructors had witnessed first-hand in Normandy, and during our withdrawal from France. Willi had also written to mother about the Americans. There was no real reason to fear them, unless you happened to be fighting them. They hated the SS, that was no secret, and by the stories Bobby had told me recently, they were not the only ones with a hatred for us. From what I could gather, there was also no love lost between us and our army guys, even though we were meant to be on the same side. I didn't want to sound defeatist, but I wasn't confident about the possibility of sanctuary, when this whole horrible war finally played out. I was dug in on a bank, not far from my own home, the enemy not too far away. What have you got yourself into here, Erik?

I felt a shove, which made me jump. Bobby was knelt over me, grinning. "You snore like a fucking freight train, boy." I made my apologies and sat up, fumbling for my water bottle. There were just a few drops left, which I gulped down. It felt good, despite the chill in the air. I was hungry, but to be fair, find me someone around here that wasn't. The stream of trudging civilians had reduced to lone individuals, and the occasional pair of sorry-looking old folk. To my right, I saw the Hauptsturmfuhrer beside a tank, talking to its panzer crew. Judging by his body language, he appeared rather agitated, facing shaking of heads, and the occasional shrugging of shoulders. He spun on his heels, and began trudging toward us. He waved for Bobby to join him. Their dialogue was muted, accompanied by nodding. It wasn't long before Bobby began rousing men from our group. We were all to convene around the Hauptsturmfuhrer.

We knelt down with him, next to his fighting position. He had a map unfolded on the ground, a crudely sharpened pencil in his hand. "The Americans have halted in Marienloh. Not too sure why; probably supply issues and the ambush threat." He began moving the pencil over the map. "We are here, just on the edge of Schlangen. Behind us is Kohlstadt. We are due to receive reinforcements. They will be moving south through Kohlstadt, anytime soon. We have been told to expect Tigers, 88s and infantry, so if you notice movement behind us, make sure you can tell who they are, before you decide to open fire, understand?"

We nodded. I was rather relieved. We would shortly be getting more troops and Tigers. We began to get to our feet, but Bobby raised a hand, waving us back down. "Hauptsturmfuhrer, what shape are our two panzers in?"

The Hauptsturmfuhrer shook his head. "They've no fuel, and only a few rounds between them. They have plenty of machinegun ammo, but not much to kill armour with."

Bobby nodded, tight lipped. Not ideal at all. The little aircraft was still loitering to the east. In fact, I vaguely remembered first seeing it from the halftrack, just north of Paderborn. "Get in your holes," barked Bobby. We looked at each other. The Hauptsturmfuhrer's face suddenly dropped from a confident glare, to one of horror. Back towards Paderborn, there was a low rumble of thunder, followed by an ever increasing screech. There was a very loud thud to the rear of our position. I turned as the blast rippled through, winding us all, punching the dust off our uniforms. I saw a huge fountain of grey smoke, along with huge chunks of earth.

There was a second screech. This time, the shell hit the road, showering gravel and mud, high into the air. The shell had landed closer to us, half the distance to the first strike. As the second blast went through us, it felt as if I'd been kicked in the testicles. The burning in my stomach was intense. "Get in your fucking holes, get away from the tanks!" Bobby roared.

I didn't need any more encouragement. I got to my feet, but the cramp in my stomach would only allow me to run at a crouch. As I got to my fighting position, another blast swept through, punching me in the back, my ears ringing. I tumbled head-first into my hole. As I got myself sorted out, I turned to see a shower of earth, raining down between the panzers. The Americans had found their mark; here it comes.

Because of the ringing in my ears, I felt the next strike before I heard it. I hunkered down in my hole, as tight as I could. The ground beneath me thudded with such force, I bounced. An impact really gave my back a pummelling. Every blast rippled over the top of me. Every time, it felt as if I was being punched in the stomach and testicles. My world was just a dust storm of punches, as if God himself was punishing me. Every time the ringing in my ears began to fade, another strike made them ring again. The biblical thuds continued, but seemed to move away slightly. Someone else had become subject to the wrath of American firepower.

As the dust began to settle, and my hearing returned, I got up onto my knees, peering out of my hole. One of the panzers was smouldering badly. I could make out broken heaps of soldiers. By the look of things, they were caught in the open. I couldn't tell who was alive; was I alone? I slowly got to my feet, dirt and dust falling from me. My skin was rough to the touch, glazed in dirt sticking to my sweat. I moved over to the nearest panzer. Its camouflage was blown clear, exposing its profile. I looked at the remnants of the other guys' fighting positions. The bank had partially collapsed, burying them in their holes. There was no evidence of anyone alive. Suddenly, the loose earth covering one position started to fall away. The profile of an arm became clear, then a shoulder, the rim of a helmet, an ear, a nose. It was Bobby, rising from the grave. I was transfixed, watching the amazing demonstration of survival. He fought halfway out, then noticed me. "Are you going to just stand there, or give me a fucking hand, boy?" At first, his words didn't register. He stretched a hand out. "Fucking help, then!" I snapped out of my trance, dashing forward. He'd managed to get his torso out from the crushing weight of soil and gravel, but I had to help him claw away at the sucking soil trap, which had his legs entombed.

It was a few minutes, before he was completely free. We lay flat on our backs, gasping for breath. We didn't speak for another couple of minutes. He had taken everything the Fuhrer had thrown at him and more, and needed time to compose himself. Then out of the corner of my eye, I saw him rooting through his pockets. He produced a very sorry looking cigarette, and placed it between his lips. "Erik, do you have a light?"

"No. Besides, those things are bad for you." We began to giggle, his laugh quickly turning to a hacking cough. He got himself onto his knees, his hands on his thighs, taking in the scene around us. I sat up, beginning to beat the dirt and dust from my smock. It fell from every crease in my uniform. He looked no better. We stood up, taking turns to beat loose soil from our equipment and uniforms.

I heard a squeaky creak of metal, and spun around. The top hatch of the closest panzer was open. A set of hands appeared above the hatch periscopes, and then a head appeared, followed by the black-clad, sweaty, dusty frame of a crewman. He scrambled out onto the back engine decks, hiding behind the turret. Bobby let out a short, sharp whistle, which caught his attention. "Guys," the crewman said quietly," the Americans are literally straight down the road. I've seen armour, but no infantry. I've got nothing to fire at them, bastards!"

We made our way towards the panzer, but it suddenly lurched back on its running gear with an almighty thud, huge sparks showering us. A piercing ring screamed through my head. I dropped to my knees, cupping my ears. The crewman was rolling around in the grass behind the vehicle. He was smouldering, one of his legs a ragged mess, his face all bloody. The panzer lurched with another muffled thud, more sparks showering the area. I lay on my belly. I saw Bobby dash over to the burning crewman. The crewman grabbed Bobby's dusty black tunic, a pleading look on his face. Bobby nodded frantically, gripping his wrists, pulling his hands. My hearing returned. The crackling of the burning vehicle was the first thing I heard. Bobby scrambled over to me. "Grenade, give it to me." I looked down at my belt kit. I had two potato mashers tucked into it, that I'd picked up since Paderborn. But in my punch-drunk state, I couldn't decide which one to give him. His patience was short at best, so he grabbed one, and scampered over to the panzer. As he prepared the grenade, his intentions quickly dawned on me. Burning crewmen were screaming inside the tank; a sound no man should ever have to hear. He scrambled up the bank, and hopped onto the vehicle. Leaning as far as the rising flames would allow, he dropped my grenade into the hatch.

Suddenly, the front of the tank was splashed in tracer bullets, which screamed and bounced in all directions, some flicking down into the bank.

Bobby was a slumped mass of dusty black uniform; half-propped on the hull, half on the mantlet of a mounted gun. I scrambled to my feet, wiping tears from my grimy face. "Fuck you," I roared, "fuck you all!"

I turned and ran, hugging the bank. I didn't look back. The Americans could be on the position, anytime now. They wouldn't give even a lone SS soldier any quarter, so why take the chance? I just kept going. The raised road would take me into the Teutoburg Forest, I knew that much. I had to get away. I didn't want to die; not today, not tomorrow, not for anyone, not for the fucking Fuhrer, not for the Fatherland, not for no fucker. What have you got yourself into here, Erik?

Part Two: The Werewolves

Chapter Eight – The Farmhouse

I hadn't gone too far, when I started to run out of steam. My lungs ached as they tried to draw in the cold afternoon air. My legs felt like they weighed a ton, my damp stockinged feet rubbing raw inside my boots. I slumped into a long ditch at the side of the road, well north of the panzers and the bank. Ahead, the road stretched off in an almost perfect straight line, reaching far into the Teutoburg Forest. Huge thick trees already formed a boundary on both sides of the road, but there was no fear of me leaving the sanctuary of the ditch, anytime soon. The tree boundary was fairly thin, open farmland beyond on both sides. Attempting to cross open fields in daylight would be as good as suicidal; the Americans must have arrived at the bank by now, to admire their handiwork.

I blundered down the long ditch, cursing under my breath. How on Earth were we supposed to stop the Americans with tanks that had no fucking fuel, no ammunition? Where was our precious fucking Luftwaffe? Where the hell was our artillery? Why were we even fighting now? Bobby's hometown had been overrun, which put the Russians close to Berlin. What was the Fuhrer expecting us to do? Max had drummed the importance into us of continuing to fight. If we surrendered, our mothers and sisters would become whores for the Russians. Don't get me wrong, I was not in favour of testing Max's theory at the moment, but surely the madness must end soon. There couldn't be much left of Germany to capture.

And what about after the war? All the talk of Jews, and our exploits in Russia. What would come of it? Would we all be held to account? Would all SS be sent to Siberia? I hadn't heard any of the tales of our exploits until recently. Otherwise, how the hell could I know what was going on in fucking Russia? Would I be sent to Siberia? Mother would be heartbroken. All her sons lost to the war. Willi in France last year, and we hadn't heard anything from Manfred in Russia for months now. Was mother still at the house? I sure hoped she was safe, hoped she had not been turfed out into the streets by the Americans, to join those fleeing the fighting. Our cellar was strong; she must be living down there, surely. I wanted to go home.

Thoughts of my own preservation raced through my head. It was selfish, I know, but all those who stood for what was good in Germany were now either dead or captured, those of us remaining about to be branded criminals. The road started a long slow climb into the hills. March had just turned to April, and the light was failing, the boundary tree canopy making it prematurely darker.

As I crested what turned out to be a false horizon, I was confronted by the hilly forest, and a rather random and bizarre sight. Fallen trees. This would not be out of the ordinary in any forest, but these were lying across the road, side-by-side. A roadblock, perhaps. I was no lumberjack by any stretch of the imagination, but whoever did the cutting was clearly not a man of the woods. The handiwork was poor, either through lack of skill or proper tools. Beside the ditch, the bases of the trees were badly hacked, splintered in a very messy fashion. The source of the cut down trees alternated; a tree from one side of the road, then one from the other side. Judging by the paleness of the insides of the trees, they had been cut recently, although I was no expert. It had to be a roadblock, there could be no other reason for the downed trees. But who had constructed it? Did we have units positioned on the hills? I wasn't sure to be relieved or scared by the thought. Would they welcome me as an extra pair of hands, or treat me as a deserter?

I had to climb out of the ditch to avoid huge clusters of branches. I began skirting round the roadblock, through the woods. I had considered clambering over the fallen tree trunks, some of which were very wide, but I didn't have the energy for that. I stood still for a moment to catch my breath, scanning through the woods, trying to pick up signs of life. If there were troops in the area, their battlefield discipline was excellent. Besides the chopped down trees, there was nothing to give away human presence. Way off in the distance, back towards

Paderborn, I could still hear the dull echo of tank fire. Some of our guys still had some fight in them. Content I was alone, I found the ditch again, and continued climbing towards Berlebeck.

It wasn't long before I'd crested a hill, and began to sweep downwards. I took a decision to walk on the road, since trudging through the ditch and woods had really sapped at my legs. Walking on the road felt great. The crunch of gravel under my boots echoed in the now closed canopy, reaching over the road from either side. Quietly confident the Americans would not scream up behind me, I took time to take stock of my current predicament. With the exception of two grenades, I was unarmed. Not much to fight with, but it was all I had. Growling in my belly confirmed lack of food. I had no water either, my thirst growing with each passing minute. It was getting cold, but walking kept it at bay for now. I was a tired, smelly, dirty mess, but nothing a bowl of hot water wouldn't cure. I was confident the good citizens of Berlebeck would help out a young soldier. They probably wouldn't arm me with weapons, but a bite to eat, some coffee and a bath would be a gift from the gods.

As the last of the light faded, I just made out a profile of buildings. No lights were to be seen, not even candlelight. The first small houses were tucked into the trees; no people, no livestock making a noise. I could hear light trickling of a stream to my right. With caution, I made my way towards it. It grew louder until I was almost standing in it. Kneeling down, I cupped my hands to scoop myself a mouthful. It tasted okay to me, so I kept drinking until I had my fill, then filled my water bottle. I was tempted to strip for a crude wash, but if I ventured a bit further into town, I thought I might find some better ablutions. I moved back onto the road and continued on. After a short time, it dawned on me that much of the place was as good as deserted.

I made a decision to break into one of the houses. Spoilt for choice, I just chose one nearest the road. I slowly picked my way over, the light as good as gone. My night vision really had its work cut out, since the overhead trees kept ambient light out. As I approached what appeared to be a front door, I could just make out the profile of a tractor, and some kind of plough. I carefully made my way to the front wall of the house. All the window shutters were closed. I almost tripped over a set of wooden cellar trapdoors. Carefully, I made my way around them, and up steps to the front door. I crouched. With caution, I took hold of a large bulbous handle, and gave it a slow twist. The door was unlocked. It creaked, as I slowly pushed it open. Before sneaking in, I felt I should announce myself at the threshold, just in case I came across a heavily-armed scared farmer. "Hallo," I called out. No answer. "Hallo, anyone home?" Nothing. I straightened myself up, confident no one was going to blast me. I took care, as I made my way down a corridor. My night vision was trying to adjust to even less light inside the house, but all appeared rather orderly. Everything was where it was intended to be; no sign of a hasty departure. Ahead of me was a heavy curtain. It covered a doorway. I put my hands forward, touching the thick rough material. To me, it had the rough texture of hessian, almost sandbag material. I slowly began to push it aside.

Cold steel pressed into the base of my skull. My stomach turned over. "You need to be more careful whose house you break into, soldier," a voice said behind me.

"Sorry sir," I stammered. "I'm tired, hungry, just looking for food."

"What is your name, soldier?"

"Erik, sir," I gasped.

"Don't move, Erik," whispered the voice, "do you understand?" I nodded frantically, the cold steel rattling on the rim of my helmet. The pressure of the steel disappeared. I heard the front door close. I was now trapped, trying to control my shivering. I dared not move. I heard the striking of a match. After a few seconds, there was a soft glow behind me, which slowly got brighter. "Turn around, Erik." I cautiously turned. In the soft glow of an oil lamp, I saw a man in uniform, holding a pistol. It appeared to be a German uniform, but no badges. Unshaven, scruffy haired, he moved towards me with an outstretched hand. "Relax, Erik, I'm Thomas." He grinned. "Just being careful when meeting new neighbours."

Relief washed over me. I took his gesture, shaking his hand enthusiastically. "Hello Thomas. Fair enough, no problems."

He looked me over carefully. "Why would an SS soldier be in Berlebeck on a night like this?"

"My unit was destroyed at Schlangen. I had nowhere else to go."

His eyes narrowed. "The Americans are in Schlangen?"

I nodded. "Yes, tanks. But up until we got hit with artillery, no sign of infantry."

He looked at me sternly. "Come with me." Picking up the lamp, he led me towards the hessian material. My first attempt to see behind the material would have failed, since there was a second piece hanging behind.

He led me into what appeared to be the main communal area of the house. Basic furnishings quickly revealed themselves in the soft light given off by his lamp, and two other lamps in the room. I followed him towards another door, propped open with what looked like a large chunk of cut wood. His boots began clattering on tiles, which led me to believe we were entering a kitchen, his lamp soon confirming it. The kitchen was a basic affair; large wood table and chairs dominated the space, grounded work units covering three sides. A door I believed would lead to the garden had more of the dark material covering it, as did a window above a sink and draining board. There was a wooden door to the right, closed flushed. He opened it. I followed him down creaking wooden stairs to a basement.

The huge basement was nothing short of bizarre. Its floor space was equivalent to the entire house above, which looked pretty big. The basement was illuminated by a large number of oil lamps. Off to the right, there was row upon row of what could only be described as folding cot beds; basic frames, canvas sheets held taught under blankets. People were sleeping on some of them. To the left was a crude headquarters set-up; a large map of Germany on the wall, and a more detailed map of Paderborn and the surrounding area. Beneath the maps, a man was sitting with his back to me, wearing a set of headphones. As I moved closer, I saw his radio set. It was crackling away, muffled dialogue coming through his headset. He was scribbling furiously on a piece of paper. Wooden constructs appeared along the left-hand wall, propping up weapons. There were a mixed bag of platoon-level weapons; pistols, rifles, submachine guns, a couple of MG-42s, even a flamethrower.

Thomas caught my attention with a click of his fingers. He waved me to him. As I moved alongside him, he gave the radio operator a nudge. "Dennis, this is Erik. He was wandering like a stray by the house."

I held out my hand. Dennis eyed me up and down, before offering me his. "Why would an SS soldier be wandering about here?"

"Things have developed in Paderborn, quicker than we anticipated," Thomas replied. "When is Dieter's team due back in?"

"In the early hours. They've still got some trees to cut."

So there had been someone out there in the woods. But they had allowed me to pass unchallenged. Thomas placed his hand on my shoulder. "No point waiting for them idiots to get back. You might as well get some rest, you look like shit."

I let out a boyish chuckle. "Thanks. I must admit, it's been a while since I've had proper sleep."

He led me over to a bed in a corner. "Here, take mine. I'm on radio watch in a minute. Dennis has been glued to that thing for some time."

"Thank you," I replied gratefully. "Thank you very much."

He nodded, eyeing me up and down again. "You can get all that crap off, before you get in my bed. We need you ready to talk, first thing in the morning. Dieter will be very interested in any information you may have, with regards to Paderborn."

A feeling of dread washed through me. "Am I in trouble?"

He grinned. "No, you're not in trouble. We just need to know what the Americans are up to, that's all. Don't fret over it now. Get all that crap off, and get some sleep, okay?"

I nodded. He walked away, giving Dennis a load of abuse. I took my helmet off. It felt like an age since my hair saw fresh air. My belt kit came off without much trouble. I stripped down to my underwear, folding my clothing neatly. Despite my clothes being filthy, I placed my equipment on top of them. I didn't want to offend anyone by having my equipment sprawled all over the place. As I lay on the cot bed, it felt like the most comfortable bed in the world. I pulled the blanket over me, giving me a feeling of isolation from the rest of the world.

Chapter Nine – Deserters and Insurgents

Hushed voices tuned in, as I slowly opened my heavy eyelids. Tilting my head to the right, I slowly focused on a group of soldiers, who were taking their equipment off and placing it on their beds. I leant further over. There was commotion and dialogue, where the radio operator was stationed. As my vision improved, I could make out the profile of Thomas, silhouetted by the oil lamps. His body language was rather animated, as he spoke to a larger man. I propped myself up on my elbows. I must have had the king of sleeps. I felt rather fresh. I just hoped I was not about to be marched out into the garden, and shot because of my legendary snoring.

I felt it only polite to quickly get dressed, and thank Thomas for his hospitality. Helmet correctly wedged under my left armpit, I quickly ran my fingers through my hair, before walking confidently over to him. As I drew near, his conversation abruptly ended. I tried to apologise for my intrusion, and thank them for their lodgings. He held up a hand to cut me short. "Erik, this is Dieter. He's our commander, and director of operations. Dieter, young Erik here was wandering like a stray cat outside the house last night. He felt it wise to break into our home, so is now under our charge." He gave me a wink.

I stood to attention, heels snapping together, about to raise the customary salute, when Dieter's huge hand grabbed my right arm. I jumped out of my skin. His piercing glare and imposing frame were enough to tell me that he disapproved. "We don't do that kind of thing around here, Erik, do you understand?"

I gulped loudly. "Yes sir, my apologies."

He released his iron grip from my bicep, allowing the blood to flow again. His glare switched to Thomas. "You and young Erik here; meet me in the kitchen in a couple of minutes, okay?"

Thomas nodded. "Sure, coffee?"

Dieter grinned. Well, more of a sinister leer than a smile. "Coffee would be great. It's been a long night." He moved over to his bed, and stripped off his fighting gear. Minus his equipment, and stripped down to undershirt, braces, trousers and boots, he looked no smaller. Through his undershirt, it was clear to see he was in peak physical condition. I'm no expert, but how could a man maintain such a physique, with the lack of food around? That reminded me again, it had been a while since I'd eaten. My stomach groaned. Hopefully, I could fill it with sweet coffee, if nothing else. Thomas led me upstairs to the kitchen, daylight slowly filling the room. The cloth material covering the back door had been rolled up, the outside world breathing in. There was a soldier stood at the stove, playing chef. Coffee was on the go. A large pot on the stove was on the boil. I made out the aroma of potatoes and vegetables. On the kitchen table was crockery. A large plate in the middle had large chunks of bread on it. I wasn't entirely sure how fresh it was, but at this moment, who gave a shit? The chef turned around and acknowledged Thomas. "Johann, this is Erik. Found him last night, sniffing around here. Another pair of hands to help out."

Johann was heavily bearded, with unkempt hair. Maybe he had been one of the sleeping soldiers downstairs. Dressed in undershirt, trousers and boots, he looked me up and down, before slowly offering his hand. "So this is the Waffen SS of today? How old are you, boy?"

I stood up straight, pushing my chest out somewhat. "Seventeen."

He shook his head. "So now we are sending children to fight. Please don't take offence, young Erik. I'm sure you have the fight of Germany in your heart."

I accepted his hand. "Yes sir."

He dismissed me with a casual wave of his other hand. "No need for that 'sir' shit with me, boy. There's only one boss man around here, and it's that big ugly bastard running the show."

Dieter entered and sat at the table. "Get back to your stove, woman, and fetch me my coffee." He gestured for me and Thomas to join him. Johann rolled his eyes, and got back to his chores.

Dieter stared at me for a while. He was a huge, menacing looking character, somewhat intimidating. If he was to brush his ash-blonde hair, and shave off several days' worth of growth, he would be a recruiting poster boy for the Waffen SS. His piercing blue eyes completed the poster image in my head. "Are you hungry, Erik?"

'Yes sir. It's been so long since I've eaten."

His giant hand pushed the plate of bread in my direction. "Eat boy, it's not getting any fresher." I looked at Thomas for approval, who nodded towards the plate. I lost no time helping myself to the largest chunk of semi-stale bread, and tucked right in. Delicious. Johann gave the three of us small metal cups of coffee. He had made two jugs of coffee, leaving one with us, then taking the other down into the cellar. He left the pot to bubble away. "What unit are you part of, Erik?" began Dieter.

I slowed down my chewing to talk, and to fight off looming indigestion. "I haven't been assigned to a unit yet. I was on the Senne, training, when we got rounded up with our instructors, and marched to Kirchborchen."

Dieter nodded. "That would explain why you have no cuff title." Each SS division was awarded a cuff title, to let people know which one you belonged to. I'd yet to receive a cuff title, given the circumstances. I doubted I ever would. "Why Kirchborchen?" he continued.

I gulped down another lump of bread. "We were told the Americans were just south of there, and were advancing on Paderborn."

"Did they enter Kirchborchen?" asked Dieter.

"Yes, but we smashed them with Panzerfaust and machineguns."

Dieter grinned with an approving nod. "Good boy, Erik, but why are you now all the way out here?"

"We only had so much ammunition. Our armour was out of fuel and ammunition, so the Hauptsturmfurher in charge ordered us to withdraw."

"Withdraw?" Dieter's eyes narrowed to a glare. "To where, may I ask?"

"A few ambushes were put in, as we made our way back to Schlangen. We were told there would be reinforcements, coming down through Kohlstadt to link up with us, so we could counterattack."

Dieter's clenched jaw and huge clenched fists gave away the fact he was not pleased. "So the fucking mighty SS allowed the enemy to capture Paderborn, along with its road and rail network!"

I nodded, avoiding eye contact. "Yes sir."

"Why are you in Berlebeck?" Dieter pushed.

I looked up at him. "What was left of my unit was destroyed at Schlangen. American artillery smashed us badly, knocking out two panzers in our position, burying my group alive. I doubted the Americans would take pity on me, so I made my way up here."

Dieter nodded. "Where are you from?"

"Paderborn."

Dieter waved a dismissive hand. "I know that, boy. Where were you born?"

"Paderborn."

"What?" whispered Dieter, then leaned forward. A look of disbelief replaced his stern gaze.

"I'm from Paderborn, sir," I said, looking him square in the face. "Bad Lippspringe."

Dieter lurched back, which made me jump. He stood up, and fumbled for the cooker knob to turn off the hob. Breakfast was ready. He turned back, his massive hand outstretched. "Welcome to, shall we say, the Reichsfurher's plan B."

I stood up, taking his hand. "What do I need to do?"

He grinned. "First, eat breakfast. Second, take all those fucking badges off."

Breakfast was nothing to write home about, but the bread more than made up for it, even though it was nearly stale. It all filled my belly. The coffee was just okay, but then again, beggars can't be choosers. I sat at the table, carefully using my breakfast knife to pick away at the stitching on my tunic. Other soldiers came and went, in and out of the back garden. They didn't give me a second glance, confidently going about their routine, whatever that was. Thomas emerged from the cellar, and resumed his seat, placing his MP40 on the table. He remained unshaven, but despite his dishevelled appearance, his gun looked immaculate. Looking at his tunic, it was clear to see he had been in the SS a while, even though he had no badges. The material was rather faded, but still its original grey colour. Loose threads remained where the badges once were, indicating he must have ripped them off. The dark grey patches on his right sleeve indicated he had been awarded tank-kill badges. The horizontal strip across his wrist was where his cuff title once sat. I had to ask. "Thomas, what division were you?"

"Das Reich. I got wounded in France last year. Once my sick leave was up, they posted me to the Senne, teaching boys like you to kill tanks."

"How did you end up here?"

"While on the Senne, I heard my division was as good as destroyed, trying to get out of France, and they were going to reassign me to the Totenkopf. I thought fuck that. There was no way I was going to Russia, so I took some leave, but never went back."

"How did you avoid the military police?" I probed.

"I just went about my own business with a confident manner. People didn't give me a second glance. I was sat in a beer keller in Detmold, when I saw Dieter and a couple of the guys, one of them being Dennis. They waved me over, and it was clear they were all from different divisions, all in the same boat as me. None of us wanted to go back to our units, so we all got our heads together, agreeing that we still had to fight, but on our own terms. It was Dennis who told us about the Reichsfuhrer's Werewolf directive. He said he'd heard it when manning a radio. The Werewolves wanted volunteers with a rogue streak for adventure and trouble, but yet loyal to the Fatherland, to continue fighting the invader of our homeland, away from conventional fighting units. We thought it would be a good way to start."

I was somewhat puzzled. "What about Fuhrer directives?"

He shrugged his shoulders. "Apparently, he dismissed the idea as defeatism, claiming insurgency was admitting we had lost the conventional campaign. I'm not entirely sure we serve with the Fuhrer's blessing right now, but we have a job to do. Harass and destroy the invader. You telling us about the Americans in Schlangen has certainly raised the stakes, let me tell you. Hence why I introduced you to Dieter." It was now becoming clear. A wave of dread washed through me. Deserters turned insurgents. What was this war coming to? The rules of the game had certainly changed, but their aim stayed the same; fight the invader. "We've got a lot to do today," he said, snapping me out of my self-pity. "The roadblock needs finishing off, before we get to work tonight."

I frowned. "Work tonight?"

He grunted, giving me a sly grin. "Killing Americans, Erik, killing Americans." My stomach turned over. There could be thousands of them in Paderborn by now, with more tanks and firepower than we could ever imagine. He sensed my uneasiness. "Not all of them, mind. Sentries that wander too far, stuff like that." That sounded more like it. I quickly thought hard, getting bad thoughts out of my head; suicide charges at machineguns, tanks, and so on. Taking out stragglers, and those who were sloppy in their personal security; I could deal with that, I suppose.

I took off my tunic. I hadn't made much progress with the badges, so if you can't beat them, join them. I picked at the badges, until I could get a finger underneath, then ripped them off. I pulled out as many loose threads as I could, before putting the tunic back on. I felt scruffy, something I was not at all used to. Our instructors would have been all over us, if we had so much as a hair out of place. The carefree abandon on personal appearance was something I would have to get used to.

I heard commotion, as multiple pairs of boots clattered up the stairs. It appeared everyone was gathering in the kitchen. They were all unshaven and scruffy-haired. Some had scars on their faces. None of their tunics had badges. Yet their weapons were all clean and ready to go. I felt above my station being sat at the table, so attempted to give up my seat for one of the more seasoned guys. A firm hand on my shoulders, and a friendly mutter of 'relax', convinced me to stay seated. Dieter was the last to squeeze into the room. He picked his way through people, struggling to find a good spot to talk from. He eventually raised a hand, calling for hush. "Main effort today, guys, getting the roadblock finished. Thomas, your team will take care of that, whilst my lot will go take a look at the Americans in Schlangen. Information gratefully received from young Erik here." I felt like a right idiot sat at the table, as all the combat veterans looked at me. "It appears that we have friendly forces coming down through Kohlstadt," continued Dieter, "anytime soon to take on the Americans. So, my guys, we must ensure that if the Americans do turn up, we are not caught in the middle. We will see what they are up to, and then we can go to work tonight, on those bastards who feel they can relax in our backyard. We will get early warning of an American advance, should they decide to move up towards the roadblock." He looked at Dennis. "Are the radios good to go?"

Dennis nodded. "Yes. Battery life could be better, but they should be okay for today."

"Remember guys," Dieter began to conclude, "today is about roadblock building and information gathering. If the shooting starts in daytime, we are to get away, and pick a fight later on, okay?" Everyone nodded. "Right, then. Get your shit sorted and be outside in the next five minutes, less Dennis and Felix. They will monitor the radio here, and make sure we have no more nosey visitors." He leered at me. I felt rather uncomfortable. The clattering of chairs and boots reigned, as everyone began to go about their business.

A hand on my right shoulder made me jump. "You will replace Felix in my team today, okay?" explained Thomas.

"Sure." I was pleased to be on the roadblock task. I wasn't confident about heading back to Schlangen, anytime soon. Thomas instructed me to take an MP40 from the cellar, along with half a dozen magazines, a grenade and an axe. I would apparently have a lot of use of the axe today.

Chapter Ten – The Roadblock

I stood outside the front of the house. It was rather chilly. I chose to wear my smock over my tunic, just to keep the wind off. It did feel rather odd not to wear a helmet, almost naked even, but since no one else was wearing one, why draw attention to myself?

Dieter led his team off first. Our team stood around a little while longer, smoking cigarettes and finishing off coffee; all very relaxed and civilised.

Thomas took the opportunity to introduce me to his team. I'd met Johann. He no longer looked like a scullery maid, very much a soldier now. He looked like he could cause a lot of trouble at a moment's notice. Without the stubble, Viktor would look like a German army poster image. He was our radioman. Gerhard was short, stocky and powerful, in fine shape despite the food limitations. Handshaking and shoulder slapping finished, cigarettes were extinguished, and we then set off to our task at the roadblock.

We patrolled out of Berlebeck, the way I had come in. The early light managed to penetrate the thick, spindly branch canopy over the road. Thomas took the lead in front of Viktor, Gerhard and Johann. I played it safe, loitering at the rear. No one appeared to mind. After all, it wasn't a fighting patrol, I hoped. We slowly made our way towards the ridgeline. Daylight allowed me to tune into the environment a lot better. The ridgeline formed part of the Teutoburger Wald, and was coated in thick ancient trees. During full blossom, they would block out a lot of daylight, giving you a feel of dawn or dusk, but winter had stripped them of their leaves, which only now showed signs of sprouting. The gradient became severe. Up on the skyline, I just made out the last two of Dieter's team. Thomas kept the pace slow and steady, but it still didn't stop us from puffing and panting. I was grateful not to be wearing a helmet, since sweat was running freely down my temples, gathering underneath my chin. Now and again, I wiped it off with the sleeve of my smock, a garment I could have done without, even though it had been cold in the garden. No one else wore one.

Just short of the summit, Thomas waved us to the side of the road. "We will give Dieter and his guys a bit of a lead, before we get to work. If the Americans have any surprises for us, Dieter will be the first to know about it." Made sense to me. The other lads lost no time getting their tobacco out, savouring every moment of rest time. Their body language was relaxed. It was our neighbourhood, nice and safe. 'Relax boy," Gerhard confirmed. "The Americans are not fans of the wald. We learned that very quickly in the Ardennes. Felix said the same about the Hurtgen. The Americans are only happy if they can fight on a wide open road. Their infantry are not ones for the forest. Relax."

I nodded. I had heard of horrific winter battles in the forests. The Americans paid dearly for the battles, so did we. But if we were better in the forests, why had the Hauptsturmfuhrer explained that the master plan was to trade space for time, by regrouping in the open at Schlangen? The answer might be that we were fighting on two fronts; the Americans on one, and the Russians on the other. What have you got yourself into here, Erik?

Once the lads finished their cigarettes, we adjusted our loads and trudged on. The road wound down to the roadblock. We followed Thomas to a rather large tree. He instructed us to strip down to just undershirts, but keep our weapons slung on at all times. Axes in hand, we went to work whilst he sat with the radio, like a foreman on a worksite.

Gerhard clambered onto the first of the huge fallen trees. He reached down to help me up. I helped him chop away branches sticking up. "We want the American tanks not to see the roadblock, at least until they crest the false horizon. They are committed at around about that point, and therefore stuck in a traffic jam, you see?" I saw the method to the madness, made perfect sense to me. If they spotted the roadblock early, they could detour around it, making all our work for nothing.

Once all upward-pointing branches were gone, Gerhard inspected our efforts, adding some finishing touches. "Right, then. We now need mud." We clambered down, venturing to the side of the road. He peered into the long ditch, then jumped in with both feet, sinking almost knee deep in dark sludge. He dug in with both hands, with all the enthusiasm of a toddler, left unattended in a garden. "Perfect!" he beamed. "Don't be shy, boy, get your arse in here, and get stuck in."

I copied him, shifting mud out of the ditch. We were both plastered. The penny dropped, as I realised what he had in mind. At the splintered ends of the fallen trees, he started to use the mud to cover the protruding pale insides. "Their tank commanders would otherwise see the splintered ends first, which would give them earlier warning of the roadblock. The later they see the trees, the more time they'll have spent moving down from the false horizon, before realising an ever more awkward traffic jam is unavoidable. All crunched up together, their tanks will also be more exposed to an ambush." He gave me a mischievous wink. I joined him in the task with enthusiasm. Most of the time on the Senne, instructors had just screamed orders at us, often not explaining the reasons behind them. Usually, it had been against our better judgement to ask why, for fear of getting screamed at again. Knowing the bloody reason for the mud-smearing made me enjoy the task. If American tanks rolled into Berlebeck when I was tucked up in bed, it would not end well for me. As across the road, Viktor and Johann cut more trees down, Gerhard and I smeared their splintered ends too. At one point, Thomas called for a break. He had a flask of nice coffee to share. Muddy and sweaty, we all gathered round him, the boys smoking cigarettes, as we laughed and jeered at each other. It only seemed a matter of minutes before Thomas jokingly called us a bunch of lazy bastards, telling us to get back to work.

At the end of it all, I proudly stood back and admired our handiwork, but then to my surprise, a tree fell in the woods, one of several Johann and Viktor were beginning to fell on either side. I was out of my depth again, unable to even guess what was going on. Gerhard read my frown, and quickly educated me. "Picture the scene," he beamed with enthusiasm, his hands out in front of him, framing his thumbs and forefingers like a movie director. "The American tanks encounter the roadblock, and try to skirt around it. They go off the road, exposing their sides to our Panzerfaust. The tanks either belly out on a tree stump, or end up stuck, straddling a fallen tree. Any sudden steering, and they lose a track." Pure genius! Remind me again why our main force wasn't in the forest, and why we withdrew from the forests in the west. Oh yeah, that's right. Trading space for time.

We helped Viktor and Johann fell more trees in the woods. I don't mind admitting I preferred playing with mud. Cutting them trees was bloody hard work. My technique was all wrong. Gerhard, a seasoned woodsman, made it look easy, the bastard. Fair play to him, though. He had the patience of a saint, as he watched me clowning around with my axe. In my defence, the trees were centuries old, and bloody wide. He laughed his arse off as I sweated and cursed nature, and all those who embraced it. But after several tutorials, I started to get the hang of it. But he was still working three times faster than me, so after a while, he had enough of me almost breaking the axe, and told me to resume mud duties on the newly fallen trees.

We ended up with 36 trees in total, lying in the woods. I'd smeared some of their splintered ends with mud, by the time the last tree fell. My hands burned with calluses from my poor chopping technique. Gerhard, although rather sweaty, still looked fairly fresh. I had to ask. "Gerhard, where are you from?"

"Bavaria," he chuckled. Say no more. Probably born with an axe in his hand. "Shall we help our comrades fling mud?" he asked. It was a rhetorical question, I'm sure, since he was already making his way to Johann and Viktor. I followed him, wanting another coffee break, but far be it from me to take a break, whilst the others were still working.

With the exception of Thomas, it was all hands to the pump with the mud smearing. We were starting to lose light, so we got a move on. As we finished up, he wandered over, weapon slung behind his back, hands in pockets. "Dieter's team is on its way back. Hopefully, he can tell us what's going on in Schlangen." We made our way to our gear, spread around the radio, then moved up to the ridgeline, waiting for Dieter and his guys. But the inactivity started to give me a chill, as my sweat began to dry. I got myself dressed, my smock now a welcome addition, since a brisk breeze was now blowing. In the fading light, we sat and relaxed. They all smoked. We chatted away about some of the usual shit soldiers talk about; beer, women, the war, the Russians, the Americans and the British. But the conversation eventually became candid. It was evident everyone was trying their hardest, not to talk about family and home. Homesickness overwhelmed me. I tried my hardest not to let it show. I'm sure some of the guys had their own fears on the whereabouts and safety of their loved ones. It paid to be young in these instances. I was single, and had a fair idea mother was okay. I had no wife or children to worry about. I didn't have to fear for my wife and daughters' safety, should they fall prey to the appetites of the invaders. Judging by the age range of the guys, they had all those family worries to contend with, as well as fighting. But what have you got yourself into here, Erik?

Eventually, we became silent, deep in our own thoughts. The wind started to cut through us, making it all the more colder on the ridgeline. I heard movement at the roadblock, snapping of twigs. Dieter appeared, then one by one, the rest of his team. As they drew near, we saw steam coming off them. They were glazed in a fine shine of sweat. I wasn't too sure if it had been the terrain that made them perspire, or the pace Dieter had set, or the sheer fright of seeing so many Americans in Schlangen. We were about to find out. "Not as much traffic down there, as we originally thought," began Dieter, laying his weapons at his feet. "A few tanks, not too much infantry. We tried to see if they had occupied any of the houses, but there was nothing to indicate such a move."

Thomas led him away for a tour of the roadblock. Dieter's team remained with us, smoking cigarettes, pulling their collars up, and hunching their shoulders to fend off the chill brisk air. I didn't know them, and thought better of rather boldly introducing myself. A sudden hand on my shoulder made me flinch. My head snapped to the left. Gerhard's muddy paw was attached to me, a beaming smile on his tired face. "Gentlemen, have you met our latest recruit? This is Erik. He has been a great help in building the roadblock you see before you."

I gave a courteous nod in their direction. They nodded in return, but cigarettes and the cold were their primary concern. "Anton, Konrad, Lars," Gerhard informed me, pointing to each of them in turn, "and this handsome devil is Otto."

Otto looked at the floor, shaking his head. "Gerhard, you should be in the circus, not the SS."

Gerhard gave an enthusiastic nod. "Once this war is over, that is my next career move. I think I would make a great lion tamer." We stifled a little chuckle.

Thomas and Dieter returned from the roadblock. Dieter gathered up his weapons. "It starts right here tonight, gentlemen."

We all looked at him. I was trying my hardest not to shiver, not too sure if it was the cold, or nerves once again. "We waste darkness by going back to the house," Dieter continued. "My team, plus young Erik here, will be going to pick a fight tonight. The remainder of you will be here, ready to assist if need be, or to help us extract from any mischief, should it get too much for us. You never know with these Americans; one minute they are playing cards, the next they are unleashing hell on you, before you have time to shit yourself. Well, it changes tonight. As of now, they will not enjoy a conqueror's sleep, and they will once again fear the darkness." I peered around. Everyone's demeanour had changed. His team no longer hunched their shoulders. Everyone stood at attention, hands on their personal weapons, pushing their chests out as they took deep breaths. The cheery banter had vanished for the night, a menacing leer written across their faces. Dieter scanned around. It was growing darker fast, and his huge frame suddenly appeared all the more menacing. He slowly nodded his head. "They will fear the darkness."

Chapter Eleven – Night Raid

Dieter took the lead. Otto, Konrad, Lars and Anton fell in behind. As the new kid, I followed on again at the rear. As we approached the roadblock, I peered around towards the guys staying behind. I felt very much out of my comfort zone. I'd already grown used to the company of Thomas' team, especially Gerhard. Thomas gave me an approving nod, Gerhard a thumbs up. Viktor and Johann were too busy with cigarettes, and taking a piss against a tree. We carefully picked our way around the roadblock, through the mud, before returning to the road, heading towards Schlangen and the Americans.

The approach to the village seemed to take a very long time. It was as good as dark. Dieter led at a steady deliberate pace, halting for a break, now and then. During the halts, I strained to detect the sound of armoured vehicles, perhaps even expecting to hear foreign voices. But all I heard was the wind rushing across the road, causing the trees to lean and sway.

I slowly began to see tops of buildings and other shapes in the distance. Dieter led us into a ditch, still some way from the two stricken panzers. It was on the opposite side of the road, from the ditch I had used to run away after the artillery attack. The whole area felt strange now, the circumstances dramatically different. I couldn't help but feel a sense of pride building up.

Before, I was running for my life, but now I was back to fight for Fuhrer and Fatherland.

We got to the outskirts of Schlangen. Previously almost hidden from view, rooftops peered down through trees. I saw the burnt-out hulks of the panzers and halftrack. We dived into the first gardens, the road slowly veering away to the left. Our pace was painfully slow, as we picked our way around chicken coops and wire-strand fences. The odd chicken got rather excited, which made me all the more nervous. The last thing we needed was a fucking chicken giving us away to the enemy. Perhaps we could steal one later to complement our vague and boring diet of vegetables and potatoes.

We came alongside a large wooden outbuilding, keeping our eyes peeled, should anyone be following us. I looked at Dieter. His dark profile looked confident, as he leaned out from our hiding place. It didn't surprise me. He'd probably already patrolled here earlier. With a faint snap of his fingers, he waved us forward. We continued with caution, further into Schlangen. I expected it to be heaving with enemy forces, but it was quiet as you could imagine; still a sleepy little village.

An abrupt and uncontrolled cough caused us to stop in our tracks. Dieter waved us all to crouch. We slowly pushed away from a house, taking up positions behind a rickety wooden fence, where we crouched motionless. I didn't have much faith in the fence stopping any bullets if shooting started, but it beat kneeling on the doorstep of someone's home. I peered over the fence, trying to see around a corner, in the direction of the cough. I saw nothing, then felt movement to my right. The rest of the team had begun crawling along the fence line, so I followed. The fence was part of a cattle pen of some sort, it smelt vile. We crawled for maybe 50 metres, then stopped. I wasn't paying full attention to our direction of progress, so got a cow-shit-smeared hobnailed boot in my face. Great. As I looked up, the grinning face of Anton stared back at me. Arsehole. I propped myself up with my forearms. Dieter was at a crouch, looking over the fence. He beckoned us to follow his gaze.

Before us sat one of their tanks, about 30 metres away. I was no expert as to what a Sherman looked like in the dark, but that's what my money was on. The building to its left was occupied, the faint glow of candlelight just shining out. I just made out shadows of people in the flickering light. A gust of wind preceded a dull clatter of metal on metal, on or around the tank. As my eyes accustomed, I saw the tank was draped in some kind of sheeting. Its main gun pointed skywards, causing the sheeting to peak like a tent. The tank was not ready for action, that was for certain, but the whereabouts of its crew was uncertain, so we remained motionless, unable to do anything daring. The cold was really starting to get to me. It didn't help that someone in the house was keeping warm. Enemy soldiers? Civilians? We just didn't know.

From the rear right of the tank, a lone figure appeared in silhouette, causing my heart to race. It was probably the closest I'd come to an American, with the exception of the commanding machine-gunner of the Sherman, back in Kirchborchen. The guy here walked slowly to a corner of the house, his features starting to appear. He wasn't wearing a helmet, but I couldn't make out whether he had a weapon. He peered towards the candlelight, confirming his comrades were inside; he was on sentry duty. He drew up to some window shutters, and began to speak to someone. There was a flicker of a spark, then another. The sentry was getting a cigarette.

My stomach turned over as Dieter strolled very casually towards the tank. How the fuck did he get over the fence so quietly? I snapped my head to my other comrades. They were as concerned and animated as me. "What the hell is he doing?" I whispered to Anton through gritted teeth.

"I have no idea," he whispered back, shaking his head frantically. "It's going to get real interesting around here in a minute."

Dieter seemed in no rush. My heart was racing. I came over all sweaty, very quickly. I dared not take my eyes from the sentry. Like a blind man, I felt my way around my weapons, and made sure I had fresh magazines close to hand. Pre-battle nerves could give a man a heart attack, I was sure of it. I couldn't remember if I had cocked my MP40, when quickly loading the first round into the breech. For heaven's sake, Erik, always be ready to fight! Dieter made it to the tank, and started to lurk around its right-hand side. The sentry continued to chat, then giggle. A drag on his cigarette brightly illuminated his face, also revealing the profile of the person inside for a moment. Whatever Dieter had in mind better be quick. He knelt down, next to the tank tracks. I just made out his silhouette, as he moved slightly away from the tank. The sentry backed away from the window. Dieter stood up, and walked slowly towards him. The sentry spun around, aware of Dieter's presence. There was a strange pause, as if the sentry didn't know what he was looking at. Dieter was standing face-to-face with him. Dieter flicked an arm up with a loud snap, and a spark of light shot the sentry in the face, his face shattering in a burst of red mist, his body dropping like liquid to his knees, propped up against the front belly plate of the tank. Dieter's round had ploughed through the sentry's face, and out the back of his skull, splintering a window shutter with a loud pop. Chickens in their coops got all excited, clucking their heads off, which sounded very loud in the cold, still air. There was muffled commotion in the room, as Dieter casually walked to the wall, just to the left of the window. There was a dull crash of furniture inside, probably the tank crew getting their act together, realising they were being ambushed. I angled my weapon over the top of the fence, copying the guys around me. We put our weapons up on top of the fence, ready to fight. Dieter casually prepared a grenade, and sent it through the window, like he had all the time in the world. A squeal of panic sounded from the room, echoing around outside. A huge thud followed, the whole house rippling with concussion and echo. The stricken half-dressed survivors began stumbling through a doorway, hands on their ears, straight into Dieter's killing zone. He dropped to one knee, using his pistol to take deliberate shots into chests and faces. The Americans piled up on top of each other, almost blocking the doorway. As the echo of Dieter's shots died away, barking dogs and foreign voices began sounding nearby. We had to get out of there, right fucking now. But Dieter casually walked away, waving at us to follow. We kept low, as we scampered back along the fence line. He just strolled along, without so much as looking at us.

We fell in behind him, making our way back through the gardens, me bringing up the rear again. I spent more time looking backwards than walking, convinced the Americans were chasing us, armed with dogs. The barking reached a crescendo, but the voices faded away. I concluded they weren't following us, thank heavens for that.

We reached the road, quickly moving to the ditch on our left. We increased our pace towards the roadblock. I began sweating like a maniac, but I didn't mind one bit, as long as we were putting distance between us and the Americans.

Before long, and after a real lick of marching pace, we began to ascend the false horizon. We carefully picked our way around the roadblock, before slowly making out the profiles of Thomas' team. There was a flurry of handshakes and shoulder slapping, before everyone fell into a column, Thomas and Dieter silently taking the lead back to Berlebeck.

As we slowly trudged to the farmhouse, exhaustion was starting to get the better of me. I needed the coming sleep. It had been a very long day. I still couldn't help but look behind me, even though the Americans were distant now. Perhaps they really were scared of fighting in the forests, or maybe fighting in the dark. As expected, the farmhouse windows were blacked out. I realised it had originally made me believe the place to be unoccupied. How wrong I had been; the heavily-armed Werewolves hell-bent on causing trouble, make no mistake. We clambered through the doorway into the kitchen, a blackout curtain swinging back behind us. The kitchen soon became rather crowded, the aroma of cooking and coffee unmistakable. Semi-stale chunks of dark bread were set in a bowl at the centre of the table, weapons quickly strewn around. The demonic glares that had greeted Dieter's announcement of the raid were replaced with cigarettes and smiles, only Dieter keeping his devil mask on. "Settle down, Felix, get that coffee dished out," he demanded. Commotion died down. Grateful men thanked Felix, as he distributed sweet liquid into various cups and glasses, taken from the cupboards. Dieter raised a hand for order. "Just so we are all in the picture, especially Thomas' team, who had the rather unglamorous job tonight of manning the roadblock. Let's talk about what we have learned and achieved tonight." He paused to take a sip, his closed eyes giving away the fact he had been looking forward to the drink. "The Americans are already of the impression that the war is won, covering their vehicles, and sleeping in the houses. This reassures me that they are not ready for action, and this will be our advantage." Everyone nodded. "Tonight, however, we have changed their way of thinking, I'm sure."

"What exactly did you see?" asked Thomas.

"We didn't venture too far into town tonight. We must be patient, and pick our fights carefully. We encountered one of their tanks covered in a sheet, a lone sentry wandering about smoking, whilst his comrades rested in a house close by. We eliminated the crew, but somehow didn't take the time to disable their vehicle." All round, the menacing grins had returned. I hadn't been happy about the patrol at all, shit scared of getting ambushed. Or worse, captured. He snapped me out of my sudden self-pity. "We quickly withdrew, and the enemy did not chase us. You see, men, they are scared of the dark and the wald. They will be easy prey, mark my words." The room slowly filled with murmuring agreement, shoulder slapping, cigarettes being lit. He called for order. "Time to rest, get some food, some more coffee. We have more work and planning to do tomorrow. Thomas' team will be on the next operation. We have plenty of

Panzerfaust in the cellar. I plan for us to start killing their tanks from now on."

Everyone started to get up, gathering their coffee and weapons. I decided it was easier for me to stay put until the kitchen cleared. Eventually, only Gerhard and I remained. He frowned at me. "How did you deal with the tank crew?"

"Dieter killed them. He shot the sentry in the face with his pistol, and put a grenade into the house. He killed the remainder, as they attempted to escape."

He grinned; not a menacing leer, but he was clearly impressed. "Not bad, not bad at all. They will be shitting themselves down there." He gestured in the direction of Schlangen. I agreed with him, but I wasn't any less scared. Now, Dieter scared me more than ever. You always get a fair idea of those who walk the walk, and those who just blow a lot of hot air. Dieter looked the part, and had now confirmed he was the part. I was still overwhelmed by his lack of personal safety, as he calmly went about killing the tank crew. It made you wonder why he took the rest of us along. The guy was dangerous, not just to the Americans. "Get some rest, boy," Gerhard piped up, lifting a ladle out of a pan. "Unless you want to eat some of this boiled shit." No thank you, I decided, taking my gear down to the cellar. There was already the hum of snoring, as I adjusted my vision to the dull warm glow of the lamps. Thomas and Dieter were talking in hushed voices, before the map of Paderborn. I wasn't interested, and went in search of an empty bed. I found one with not too much trouble, making sure it didn't belong to someone else, before stowing my gear beneath. The bed creaked as I carefully laid down, pulling the blanket up over my face. What a day.

Chapter Twelve – The Party

I woke with a start. Weapons were being cocked. I sat bolt upright, only to be greeted by Otto, stripping his weapons down, placing the components on the bed next to him. A wave of relief washed over me, as I lay back down. To be caught in the cellar by the Americans would only end one way; not in our favour. I rubbed sleep from my eyes, focusing on the ceiling, not for any particular reason; it was just the easiest thing to look at in my semi-sleep state. "Erik," Otto said, "remind me never to have you in my ambush party." I peered at him with a frown, not too sure how to respond. He shook his head. "Your fucking snoring keeps the Eastern Front awake, you noisy bastard."

"Sorry," was all I could muster. It wasn't the first time my snoring had brought a verbal reprimand to my ears, first thing in the morning. On the Senne, it hadn't been uncommon for our instructors to come crashing into our barrack block for roll call, and find half the troops' boots around my bed, where they had attempted to silence me in the darkness.

Looking around the cellar, I eased myself to a sitting position. Some beds were empty, others still had occupants. Cigarettes glowed amongst those who had stayed put, a light-grey smoke column drifting upwards in various shapes. Some had even mastered blowing smoke rings. I wasn't a smoker, but how they did it fascinated me. I flung my legs over the side, and carefully slid my stockinged feet into my boots. I ran my fingers through my hair, which was getting tougher by the day. I couldn't remember the last time I had a bath or shower. No one had complained how I smelt. That was a bonus, I suppose. But my snoring did me no favours. That was for sure.

"Tell you what," Otto piped up, a cigarette now dangling between his lips, as he wiped his stripped-down weapons, "fetch me a coffee, and I will try my hardest to forgive you."

I nodded, it seemed like a fair trade. "Okay." I got to my feet, and carefully picked my way towards the stairs. The daylight from the kitchen told me the blackout curtains had been removed. I clumsily made my way upstairs. I was greeted by the sight of Thomas and Dieter, sat at the table. They were poring over a map, both armed with a pencil. "Good morning," I smiled. They stopped talking, looked me up and down, and then carried on. Charming. I spotted a coffee pot on the stove, and grabbed two tin cups. They had recently been used, but I wasn't too worried. I just wanted to quickly get drinks, then get out of there. Dieter and Thomas looked like they had more trouble planned for us, my stomach tightening in anticipation. I filled the cups, a generous helping of sugar in them.

I carefully made my way back to the cellar. Otto had finished cleaning his weapons, and was lying on his bed, enjoying another cigarette. He sat upright when I offered him one of the cups, carefully taking it from me with both hands. "Thank you, young man," he said, glad somebody was in a mood to be sociable. We drank in silence. I was never much good at small talk. Once I finished my cup, I looked down at my gear, feeling I should maybe clean it or something. I picked up the MP40, and removed the magazine from its housing, ensuring there wasn't a round in the breech. I reflected that if I hadn't loaded a round at the house in Schlangen, I would have wasted precious seconds before contributing to the fight, not that there had been any requirement; Dieter killed the tank crew on his own, before we could take in what was happening. With my weapon stripped down to its basic components, I wiped it with a cloth Otto offered me. I took my time to inspect the weapon for rust. There was none. Whoever owned this particular weapon had taken great care of it. Once content it would work, I reassembled it, ensuring the firing mechanism worked correctly, before replacing the magazine. Done. Now, I would only cock the weapon prior to going out on an operation, which I knew wasn't too far away. I checked the remainder of my fighting gear. My grenades appeared to remain serviceable. My belt kit was in an acceptable state, given the company I was in. I doubt it would have passed muster on the Senne, but those days were well and truly gone.

Heavy feet thudded down the stairs. Dieter peered over a bannister. "Get up, you lazy bastards, we've got work to do." Blankets stirred around the foul-smelling room. I felt I should get out of the way, so I made my way towards the stairs with my gear and weapons. As I took the first rung of the bannister, I noticed Gerhard on radio watch. I caught his attention with a casual wave. He gave me a wink and thumbs up, then began to scribble furiously, a muffled voice babbling away in the headset.

Trying to seek refuge in the kitchen wasn't a good idea. Troops tended to want coffee and food, first thing. So I made my way into the frost-coated garden. As I stood outside in the crisp air, I reflected that with the exception of the Werewolves in the farmhouse, the village of Berlebeck was relatively untouched by the war. I moved to the road, the commotion inside fading away. I tried to detect signs of life. Some chimneys gave away people cooking, or trying to keep warm, but there were no people to be seen. I pulled my smock tighter around me, and made my way back inside. The kitchen was crowded; everyone standing, dressed and with coffee. Thomas and Dieter stood by the stove, poised to address us. I managed to find a spot, as Dieter called for quiet. "Right, guys, the plan for today is to get the roadblock finished off. By that, I mean fighting positions. And this evening, we are going back into town, to see what we can do. We have Panzerfaust at our disposal, so I want us to start knocking out their armour. If you can kill the crew as well, even better, but our main effort must be reducing their means to fight us. With their armour destroyed, they will be even less keen to fight us in the dark, would you agree?" There were plenty of nods and murmurs. "Today and tonight, Dennis and Otto will stay here to man the radio. The remainder of us will work on the roadblock. Then at last light, we will go down into Schlangen, and see what the Americans are up to. Remember, guys, don't bite off more than you can chew. We need to ensure we can get away after an attack, understood?"

There were more nods. Thomas spoke up. "Two Panzerfaust per man. You will leave one at the roadblock, and take the other into town with you. You never know, we might get some juicy targets. Plus ensure we take enough axes for the work we need to do. Any questions?"

There were none. Without much direction, the guys formed a human chain on the cellar stairs, Panzerfaust and axes manhandled onto the kitchen table. I slung my MP40 around my body, and took the top two Panzerfaust from the pile, before making my way outside.

Before long, the men started filtering out to join me. Cigarettes were smoked, feet stamped, trying to keep out the cold. The breath from everyone was visible, mixed in with tobacco smoke. I must admit, the aroma of tobacco on a cold morning did smell rather appealing. In the Senne barrack block, I had once tried to roll a cigarette from loose tobacco and papers, but made a right cock-up of it, much to the amusement of my fellow recruits. However, the instructor who was the intended recipient of my efforts was most pissed off, as I dropped his tobacco all over the floor. It cost me a night of polishing the entire barrack's boots.

As the last of the men filtered into the garden, I noticed Gerhard and Felix venturing into one of the many random outbuildings that littered the property. Gerhard popped his head out, and with a low sharp whistle, he beckoned us over. "Here you go, boys," he said, pointing to a rusty pile of short, thin metal pickets, just inside the door. "These will do the trick, when building up our fighting positions."

Dieter nodded his approval. "Well spotted. Alright guys, grab two each. Erik, you can have that hammer over there." In the dim interior of the shed, I just made out the profile of a very sorry looking hammer. It had seen better days. Its wooden handle was black, but worn smooth. The head was coated in rust. The handle was about eight inches long, which allowed me to tuck it underneath my belt kit. I managed to get away with not having to carry any of the pickets, which suited me, since I had two Panzerfaust and my own weapons to cart up to the roadblock. Once I had readjusted myself, I was good to go. Gerhard gave me a wink and a nod to get on with it.

The pace to the roadblock was slow and deliberate. We had heavy cumbersome loads, yet had to stay alert to the presence of any Americans. The attack on the tank crew might have made the enemy exploit out of Schlangen. The Americans might have even discovered the roadblock, now laying in ambush, who knew? It wasn't long before I was sweating, breath and sweat hanging over the column of guys in front of me. At the ridgeline, we took a rest, tobacco soon filling the air again. "You guys wait here," instructed Dieter. "Thomas and I are going to check out the roadblock, for anything out of place."

They made their way, down and out of sight. Gerhard shook his head and grinned. "They would have us march to Berlin, if they had their way."

I frowned. "Really?"

He nodded. "Enjoy the war, Erik. History will not be kind to us." It sounded familiar. My thoughts drifted to Bobby. He had fought like a man who had nothing left to lose. Should I fight like that? If I resigned myself to death, would I perform better? Be more reckless? More daring? I sat in silence, listening to the quiet hum of conversation.

Before long, Dieter and Thomas returned. "The roadblock is clear," Dieter stated. "Let's go, we are burning daylight." We all clambered to our feet and trudged on. Even from a distance, the roadblock looked impressive. Yet it blended in with its natural surroundings, as if it had always been there. Cold and wind had helped disguise it a little more.

At the roadblock, Thomas and Dieter acted as foremen, as we split into pairs to establish our fighting positions. I stuck with Gerhard. I liked him, and knew I would learn a lot of stuff from him. He took his time siting our fighting position, in the woods to the right of the roadblock. "We need a clear shot at the side of their tanks," he explained. "I don't want our rockets clipping branches and trees, on the way in. We also need to have a strong enough position to fend off their infantry, who will no doubt be in the woods, on either side of the road. Our rocket shot will be a one-shot deal. Their tanks will not allow us a second chance if we miss."

We chopped smaller, thinner trees, from way back in the woods, not wanting to add to the impression of human interference around the roadblock. We chose thin trees, because it was easy to drag them to our position for carving and shaping. The pickets helped us stack logs, reasonably high. Gerhard didn't want them stacked too high, however, since it would look out of place, making it impossible to conceal our position.

My undershirt was sweaty when we finished. We stood away from our position, admiring it. The logs stacks were thigh-high, hard to detect from the road. Content, we began smearing the logs with mud. "What if their infantry are real close when the ambush is sprung?" I asked.

He looked at me deadpan. "Don't be a hero, Erik. Throw your grenades, spray a full magazine at them, and then run!" Fair enough. We made our way back to where our gear was located. Dieter and Thomas were deep in conversation, not even acknowledging our presence. It was a clear day, still bloody cold. The other pairs hadn't finished, and there had been no mention of going to help them. I sure as hell wasn't going to suggest it. Unlike me, they were all experienced enough to prepare ambush positions. I hadn't even officially finished recruit training.

It was another hour or so, before they all finished cutting wood. It was mid-afternoon, and we were already starting to lose daylight. I wondered if I would ever again feel the warmth of a summer on my face. The winter had been one of the longest and harshest I had ever known. But I guessed we had it easier here, than in the east. Thomas called for quiet. "Shortly, we are going back into Schlangen. We are all going. The aim of tonight's mission is to knock out as many of their tanks as possible. If we find other targets that are too good to miss, we will deal with them too. Your Fuhrer demands that you are ruthless with the invader. Give them no quarter, allow them no respite from this war. They are sitting down there, like their war is over, but let me assure you of this; theirs is only just beginning." With the exception of Gerhard, the sinister leers on everyone's faces had returned. He remained deadpan; nothing sinister, just professional. "The darkness is ours, comrades," concluded Thomas. "They will fear the darkness."

'They will fear the darkness,' everyone else chanted back. The Sun was going down fast. My stomach tightened with nerves, doubting my own position amongst the group. By day, they were soldiers with hopes and dreams, laughing and joking at each other's misfortunes. But by night, they became something else. Not monsters, but detached from humanity and decency. They would do whatever it took to win the war. Even if Germany couldn't win, they sure as hell were going to make the invader pay. What have you got yourself into here, Erik?

It was as good as dark when we finally set off. I thought I would freeze, if I stood around any longer. My feet ached badly in my boots, my stomach knotted with hunger and nerves. I wasn't in the mood to drink cold water. I just wanted to get on with what was on the cards tonight; tank hunting. If the other lads were as cold as me, they never let it show. They were in another place right now. The sinister grins and glares on their faces gave away their readiness to inflict pain and mayhem on the Americans. I wasn't entirely sure which team I was with for this one. I kept it simple in my head; I would go where Gerhard went.

A fog settled, the night air even colder. As the treeline started to thin out, we moved to the left-hand ditch. The fog got somewhat thicker, closer to Schlangen. Some guys cursed as the ditch became muddier, so we moved into a fog-laden field. We moved carefully through the fog, with the bank of the road to our right, and nothingness to our left. There could have been a whole battalion of Americans, sat beyond the fog. We wouldn't have seen them, nor they us. Fear began to build up in my mind, trying to take my breath, but I managed to keep the fear down within me. Just do what the others do. If they were scared, I just prayed they could hide it too. We halted. The guys up front got down on their bellies, weapons ready for action. I followed their example, on my belly on the cold grass, looking out into the thick fog. I saw nothing. I heard whispers from up front, getting louder and louder. Felix was in front of me. "Two vehicles up front," he informed me, "people moving about. 50 metres." My stomach turned over. We had walked right in amongst the Americans. It would be a slaughter if our presence became known. How could we have not noticed them earlier? My mind was racing, building up an image of hundreds of enemy looking at us, waiting for the order to destroy us all. I hated the fact I couldn't see them. If you could see them, at least you stood half a chance of fighting back. What the hell were Thomas and Dieter thinking? I cursed them for their fatal error. Fancy speeches before a mission, and this was the result. Assholes!

Up ahead, the guys began to get to their feet, moving forward. Were they nuts? Even those behind me were standing up, madness! Felix gestured for me to follow him. I scrambled to my feet. Shapes began to materialise on the bank, along with a foul, sweet smell. What on Earth was it? Out of the gloom came the profile of a tank. Dogs were giving out low snarls, pulling at something on the front of the turret. It then hit me. They were eating Bobby. Burning bile rushed up my throat, but I managed to keep it down. The burning sensation was intense, as I fought not to choke. The dogs were eating our dead. What was the world coming to? Why had bodies not been recovered? But then something else hit me. Why would the Americans care about our dead? They had their own to deal with, I was sure. As we got closer to the tank, the dogs scampered away into the fog, back towards town. I just hoped they wouldn't alert any Americans nearby. We clambered up the broken bank. I knew it might contain those buried alive during the artillery assault. I peered over the top, then laid down beside Gerhard. The fog seemed lighter. I strained to see Schlangen. I couldn't see any people moving, but I did see what appeared to be laundry, flapping from almost every window. People still occupied the houses, then. I couldn't see any military vehicles. I made out the clucking of chickens, and a crying baby.

We stayed on the bank for a while, trying to get a feel for the situation in Schlangen. The smell from the bank was vile. I knew exactly what was rotting, but now was not the time to share the information. The cold grew even more intense. I wasn't the only one feeling it. Even the hardest men were shivering. Whispers emanated from my left. "We are crossing the road," Felix told me, "going into town from the left side. Pass it on." I told Gerhard, who nodded, turning to the guy on his right.

A few minutes later, we carefully got to our feet. The lads up front walked calmly across the road, and down the opposite bank, making a line for some buildings. We lined up along the side of a house, tuning into the area, before moving on. The sounds were still nothing out of the ordinary; babies, barking dogs, excited chickens. We began moving through the streets, nice and slow with a lot of stop and start, those up front taking care at every corner. In one quiet street, there were a lot of white bed sheets hanging from the windows, more so than elsewhere. Was it laundry day or something? We went firm along the wall of a house, but then someone at the front wandered into the middle of the road. Who the hell was it? I quickly identified the profile as Dieter, the biggest guy in our group. He casually wandered off into the fog, as if he was on his way home from work. Last time I saw him stroll away so casually, he killed a tank crew single-handed. He scared me. The lads became restless, beginning to question his motives. Thomas came down the line to keep proper order. There was clearly a reason for Dieter's rather brash move, but I couldn't think of one. I was cold, scared, our leader bloody wandering off. But before long, a lone figure casually strode through the gloom. Dieter stopped right in front of me. Rather loudly, he asked for everyone to gather round. It was too weird. He looked furious. He stood on tiptoe, grabbing a large white sheet flapping above us, ripping it down. "The good people of Schlangen appear to have surrendered, hence the fucking bed sheets from every fucking window. The cowardly vermin. How the fuck are we to continue to fight the invader, when our own people give up?" His temper was fraying, his voice getting louder. I was starting to get that nervous feeling again. "Tonight, we will make an example of someone for this treachery," he warned, "mark my words. Let's go!" He stormed to the front of the column. Everyone fell in behind him. We moved down the street at a rather steady pace, unlike the earlier cautious moves. I think I could safely say there were no Americans nearby, at least I hoped there weren't. We began to make our way through gardens and outbuildings, at a more cautious patrol pace. I just hoped Dieter's anger didn't get the better of him, putting us in a grim situation, surrounded by the enemy. We entered a maze of wire-strand fences, chicken huts and more outbuildings. The column stopped suddenly. I could just make out the sound of music. I thought my mind was playing tricks on me. But others agreed it was music. Word came down the line to stay put. Dieter and Thomas were going for a closer look. We all got down on one knee. Our current position wasn't good at all; not much for cover, overlooked by various houses. If any of the houses were occupied by Americans, it would only take one to go for a piss in the garden, and it would all go really wrong, really quickly.

It felt like hours, but must have only been a couple of minutes, when Thomas and Dieter returned. In a quiet and controlled manner, they called us to gather round. They looked pleased. I wondered if I should start to worry. "There appears to be a drinks party going on," whispered Thomas, "just through the houses there. There are tanks, but they are covered over, not ready for action. Their crews could well be in these houses." He pointed at the houses overlooking our position. My stomach turned over. It would just take one guy to go for a piss. "It must be some of their brass having the party," Thomas continued to whisper. "There are three jeeps parked outside. Their drivers are looking rather cold and bored, so won't be ready for us." He grinned menacingly.

"What are we to do?" whispered Gerhard.

"Ignore the tanks," Dieter jumped in, "they are not a threat at this point. We will have two groups. Mine, including you and Erik, will hit the house party with the rockets. Thomas's team will deal with any emerging enemy. Once we've put the rockets into the house, we will run for our lives, straight up the street, towards where we encountered the dogs, clear?" There were nods all round. It seemed straightforward enough. "My team, make sure you have your Panzerfaust ready for action. We need to hit them quickly, to have the desired effect. Their tanks will not race down here in the dark, if they hear rocket fire. It will be too risky for them. But their infantry might be upon us real quick, so be on your game." The lads dispersed at a crouch, everyone fearful of Americans looking down from the houses. I quickly prepared my Panzerfaust for action. I also ensured my MP40 was to hand, my magazines and grenades ready to go. I forgot the cold. I had more pressing issues at hand; imminent combat.

Dieter led us very slowly between the houses, towards the music. The alleyway was very dark, which gave me comfort. Commotion was coming from a house to our left, just out of sight. None of us spoke, there was no longer a need for it. The commotion was accompanied by the rustling sound of a cold fabric smock, together with the odd scrape of boots on a concrete pathway. We remained in the alley for some time, Dieter peering around the corner, now and again. Thomas sometimes leaned out further, confirming targets.

"Panzers," whispered Thomas. Dieter snapped his fingers, calling his team forward. We followed him slowly and cautiously across the road. With the best will in the world, we couldn't silence our boots on the cobbled street. Four tanks were parked up to our right, facing north out of town. They were covered up. Their crews could be in any of the houses on the street. It was getting too much to bear.

Dieter carefully led us through small front gardens, until we reached the last one on the terrace. The music had grown louder. He peered around a corner, nodding. "We will line up along the fence," he whispered, pointing to a fence, separating a garden from the road. "You'll see three jeeps from there, with three drivers." He grinned. I was shitting myself. "Ignore the drivers. Put the rockets through the front door, and the large window on the right. As you'll see, the lights are on, people moving about inside. Get into position, don't rush. I don't want the drivers giving us away." On my knees and forearms, I slowly made my way to the fence. I heard my heart beating loudly. I was soaked in sweat, despite the short slow movements. Once in position, I saw the jeeps easily. The drivers stood between them, hands often in pockets. Every now and then, their faces glowed with the drag of a cigarette. Dieter crawled down the line, taking a knee just behind me. He put a heavy hand on my shoulder, which almost gave me heart failure. "Steady lad, you are shaking like a leaf." I thought I was okay, but clearly my nerves were evident. Across the road, I noticed Thomas' group, getting into position in the opposite gardens. To me, they sounded like a herd of elephants in the cold still night, but I was getting hyper-sensitive. Thomas gave the thumbs up. Here we go. "Get ready," whispered Dieter. I focused on the large window, its curtains partially closed. Uniformed figures moved backwards and forwards in the softly-lit room. Laughter echoed out into the street. The music seemed to get louder. Ignore the drivers, Dieter had told me. "Stand up," came a whisper. My legs burned, as I slowly got to my feet, both hands on my Panzerfaust. I put it on my shoulder, ready to fire. I caught a glimpse of a young girl in the window, handing out drinks. I blinked rapidly. But there she was, laughing and smiling.

"FIRE!" roared Dieter.

As we fired our rockets, the thud overwhelmed me. I saw a snatch of the girl's horrified face, as rockets ploughed through the window, tremendous explosions rippling down the street. The drivers were smashed full-on. Ringing in my ears began to muffle out noise. As the noise subsided, my hearing began to return. But straightaway, I became rather confused. Dieter ran full sprint at the house. He finished the drivers off with his pistol, shattering their faces, almost deliberate execution-style. Then he disappeared into the house. What the hell was he doing? The streets around us were filled with the sounds of crying babies, men shouting, chickens going mad, the spluttering of tank engines coming to life. We really need to be getting out of here, right fucking now.

Dieter came back out onto the street, waving us over to him, and waving over Thomas' group. What the hell was happening? We jogged over to Dieter. "We have prisoners," he announced. I couldn't believe it.

"What fucking prisoners?" demanded Thomas. "We are not here to fuck around, Dieter." The commotion in the streets around us was getting louder. The Americans would be all over us in a matter of minutes.

"We have a male and a female we can use to our advantage," Dieter stated. "We will send a strong message to those who invade us, and collaborate with the enemy."

"What the fuck are you talking about?" gasped Thomas. Dieter waved for Thomas to join him inside. Thomas beckoned me and Gerhard to follow. We made our way into the hallway. The right-hand wall was shattered and smouldering. The wooden staircase was badly splintered, a narrow strip of carpet running up the centre smouldering badly. We followed Dieter into the first room on the left. The entire room was a mess of shattered furniture and glass. The curtains were smouldering. There were a small number of what appeared to be dead Americans. One was alive, propped against the back wall. He wore shirt, trousers and boots, breathing heavily through a bloodied face. A badly-bloodied woman was alongside him. Her dark dress was badly torn, her hands on her ears. Was this the girl I saw, just before we fired? Above us, probably in the bedrooms, I could make out the sound of crying children. What a horrible time for them. I felt terrible. What have you done, Erik?

"Stand up!" Dieter roared at the girl and the American. "Stand the fuck up!" They sat there looking at him. She let out a squeal of agony, as Dieter grabbed her hair, dragging her to her feet. "Are you deaf?" he roared in her face. "You Jew fucking whore."

"She can't fucking hear you!" Thomas shouted at him. "Look at the blood coming from her ears." Sure enough, she was in a bad way. Still on the floor, the American was in no better state. Thomas grabbed him by the shirt, dragging him up. Blood was also pouring from the American's ears. He was in no condition to resist.

"They come with us," ordered Dieter, glaring at Thomas.

Thomas glared back, and then after glancing at the American, he shoved him at Gerhard and me. "Get him outside," Thomas barked, "he will be coming with us." We firmly hustled the American outside. The cold air took his breath away. He was the first American I'd seen up close. Very much human, now just our prisoner, not the broad-chested movie star I had imagined as a boy. The streets sounded like chaos. I heard distant foreign male voices, vehicle engines, the rumbling squeal of tank tracks, dogs going berserk. We had to leave right now, or we weren't leaving at all.

Thomas and Dieter came outside. Dieter still had the girl by her hair. She was groaning and sobbing, a real mess, holding his wrist with both hands. She wasn't very tall. He was a colossus in comparison. The blood on her face was beginning to dry and flake, streaks of tears cutting through the blood on her cheeks, making her face look even worse. "You and your team take him," Dieter very authoritatively ordered Thomas, "and get back to the roadblock. My team and I have one more thing to do, before we leave. Go now." Thomas nodded, a look of contempt for Dieter on his face. Thomas took the American from us, shoving him over towards Johann and Lars. The prisoner stumbled, and fell to his knees with a groan. Lars and Johann pulled him roughly to his feet. Thomas took the lead, as they marched off towards the alleyway with their prisoner. Dieter peered down at the girl. "You little Jew fucking whore, you are about to serve the Fatherland in a manner befitting your crime." She was sobbing too much for me, her pleas very loud. She could still very well be deaf from the ambush. He sneered at her, then flicked his head to us. "Let's get the fuck out of here!" It was the best decision he had made all night.

    Gerhard led us back to the alleyway. We had wasted too much time to just run north, straight out of the village. There was an almighty thud of grenades in the gardens beyond the alleyway, followed by heavy chattering gunfire. Had Thomas' group been ambushed? Gerhard waved us to stay put, moving through the pitch-black alley to investigate. The girl was sobbing even louder. Dieter grabbed her by the throat, talking through gritted teeth. "Shut your fucking mouth, whore!" Why did he bother? She probably couldn't even hear him. Gerhard waved us forward, leading us into the gardens. I followed quickly. It didn't occur to me that he might be leading us into an ambush, I just trusted him. As we made our way through the gardens, we encountered two bodies, both American. They were half-dressed, face down in the mud, probably from a tank crew billeted in the nearest house. We pressed on, the sound of chaos in the streets getting even fucking louder. You would be forgiven for thinking that every household owned at least one dog. But it quickly crossed my mind that they might be American army dogs, tasked with following our trail. I was just scared, wanting to get back to the roadblock as quickly as possible.

Gerhard slowed the pace down, as we approached the edge of the village, where I had first seen bed sheets swaying in the heavy fog. I felt a little more confident on the road leading out of town. In the open, fog slowed everything down. I could still hear tank engines, and the squealing of tracks on cobbled streets, but the crews would now be very wary of Panzerfaust teams, lurking in fog and shadows. Even enemy infantry would move around with caution, not wanting to get ambushed by us, or take friendly fire from one of their own patrols. The fog had made everything look really spooky before, but now I started to take comfort in it.

My little world instantly shattered, when probably from a street to our left, a volley of tank and machinegun fire sounded. Tracer flicked skywards, glass smashing, tile and bricks collapsing. What the hell was going on? I couldn't help but look at Dieter for some inspiration, as he struggled with the girl along the road. "They are shooting at their own shadows," he said. "Keep fucking moving, boy!"

I wasn't going to argue with him. I turned, and kept my gaze upon Gerhard, who was hopefully leading us to safety. We carefully crept our way through gardens at a painfully slow pace, trying not to excite dogs or chickens, knowing they might give away our position to the Americans. But the girl's sobbing became horrendously loud. The sound of a sharp slap across her face, followed by a high pitched squeal, made me wince. Why were we taking her with us? The thought of her rape suddenly filled me with dread. The girl was German, for Christ's sake. What the hell were we doing, attacking our own people? It wasn't right. The world was crazy enough without shit getting thrown in too, but what could I do?

We finally made it to the two stricken panzers on the bank, where the dogs had been eating Bobby's remains. Gerhard peered back down the road. The whole area was slowly quietening down. Dogs still barked, but the sound of enemy armour in the fog had almost gone, and I couldn't hear voices anymore.

Chapter Thirteen - Backlash

Dieter made his way forward to Gerhard, still dragging the girl by her hair. "Gerhard," Dieter said, "I want to leave a little gift for the Americans, and anyone who wishes to collaborate with them." He pulled her upright, making her cry out.

Gerhard's eyes narrowed to a glare. "Dieter, I am not in the business of punishing our own people. Fighting the enemy, yes, but what we are doing right now, is not how it should be done."

I took this as my cue to side with Gerhard. "I'm not raping anyone, I don't care who you are. This is wrong, Dieter, let her go!"

Dieter looked me up and down with a menacing grin, and a nod of his head. "I admire your balls, boy, I'll give you that. But if you are too squeamish for what is going on around here, then you'd better run back to your mother's tit."

I felt anger building up in me, but I knew I was no match for him. It was evident he had killed bigger and better men than me, but there was no need for the girl to be caught up in this. I felt myself welling up slightly. "Let her go, Dieter," demanded Gerhard, "she is of no use to us."

Dieter rolled his eyes, his expression sarcastic, dismissing him out of hand. "Gerhard, be a good German." He raised his MP40, gesturing towards the stricken panzers on the bank. "Take the boy with you, over to where the dogs were. Wait for me there. Is that order too much for you to understand?" His sarcastic facial expression became a sinister glare. He pointed his weapon at Konrad and Anton. "You two come with me, or have you also got something to cry about?" They slowly shook their heads with menacing grins. Their loyalty to him was evident.

Gerhard slowly made his way towards the bank, his furious glare fixed on Dieter. Gerhard then flicked his gaze to me, and after another flick of his head, I followed him. Once up on the road, I turned to see profiles of Dieter, Anton and Konrad, dragging the girl into the fog. My heart went out to her. I dreaded her fate, and cursed myself out loud for not helping her. I felt my eyes well up again. I looked at Gerhard, who had returned to his deadpan expression; no emotion, he just stared into the fog. "What will happen to her?" I managed, whilst fighting the urge to sob.

"He wants to leave the Americans a message, and anyone who cares to interact with the enemy."

"Will they rape her?" The whole image of it turned my stomach.

"No, Dieter is too angry for that." It reassured me slightly, but I still dreaded the outcome for her. "Did you see how angry Dieter was," continued Gerhard, "when he ripped the bed sheet down? Schlangen has capitulated to the enemy, hence the white sheets hanging from every bloody window."

"What does it all mean?"

"Germany is dying."

I turned, and looked down the bank. The bloated, foul-smelling remains of Bobby were still slumped over the main gun. The dogs had done a good job on him. They had eaten pretty much most of his face, his skull clear to see. His black panzer suit was in shreds, where they had forced access to edible parts of his body. Gerhard joined me. "This was my last position, before I found the roadblock," I told him. "I knew this man."

"Where was he from? Did he have family?"

"Frankfurt on the Oder. He fought on because he heard the Russians had overrun the town. He talked of his wife and daughter."

He slowly nodded. "Dark times, my friend. But the Sun will very soon shine again, I promise you that. It will shine again, one way or the other." I believed him. There couldn't be much resistance left in Germany. What was left to throw at the Americans, the Canadians, the British and the Russians? The only thing I could think of was Dieter. It sounded ridiculous, but if every town across Germany had one Dieter in it, it might be enough to keep this horrible war going on, just a little bit longer.

Footsteps behind us snapped me out of my self-pity. Dieter, Konrad and Anton appeared from the fog at a jog. As they climbed the bank, steam from exertion lifted from them. Their faces were glazed in a shine of sweat. My stomach turned over. Had they raped her? "We will stay here 'til first light," declared Dieter. "I want to see that people get the message."

"What have you done?" Gerhard demanded.

Dieter spun on his heels, putting himself nose-to-nose with him. "I have ensured that whoever collaborates with the enemy will fear the same fate, understand?"

Their eyes locked for what felt like forever. I wanted to split them up, but Anton stepped in. "Enough of this," he said. "We are meant to be soldiers. Get your shit together, both of you." Dieter and Gerhard slowly stepped away from each other, still glaring. Dieter scrambled down the bank. We all followed him, Gerhard last. We spread out along the bank. The cold seemed more evident, my smock offering little respite, as I began to calm down. There wasn't anything to wrap around myself. I found myself a semi-decent fighting position. I didn't have a digging tool, but that suited me just fine. I didn't want to dig up one of the guys buried by the artillery assault. I made myself as comfortable as I could. I placed my MP40 and grenades on the bank, facing upwards. The other lads had also laid their weapons out. I didn't like Dieter's idea of sticking around until dawn, fearing being caught in the open. This close to the village, only fog and darkness had enabled us to remain undetected. Dawn wasn't far away now. If the fog lifted at first light, we would be in full view of the Americans. Not good.

My thoughts turned to Thomas and his team. Had they made it back to the roadblock? What of their prisoner? What use was he to us? The Americans were hardly going to leave the area, just because one of theirs had been taken. Let's be fair, both sides had come too far to let something like that disrupt the war. We were losing, that was evident to see, and now merely playing for time. What of the supposed reinforcements from the north? Would they come at all? Maybe they had been sent elsewhere, or destroyed by enemy fighters. Who knew? Were the Russians in Berlin? How would we know? Would those in command even tell us? If the enemy had Berlin, would we fight on? What would that achieve? More people dying, that's all. What would happen when the fighting was over? What would become of Germany? Would we become slaves to the conquerors? Was that why we were still fighting? Were we fighting for the survival of Germany? Or for the survival of the

Fuhrer? We learned at school that he had done great things for Germany. So how had it all come to this? Paderborn smouldering on the horizon, enemy troops there, with me dug in on a mud bank, waiting for them. What have you got yourself into here, Erik?

My thoughts were interrupted by a loud echoing scream. What on Earth was it? I looked at Gerhard, catching his eye. He slowly shook his head. What was going on? Movement to my left caught my attention. Dieter slowly crawled up the bank, peering over the top, the first pre-dawn light coming to life, the fog indeed starting to lift. We all crawled up to join him. The road into Schlangen was still heavy with fog, but I could make out movement on it. A pair of streetlamps marked the edge of the village. They had probably remained unlit, throughout our demise. There were people stood beneath one of them, a mixture of soldiers and civilians. Some of the civilians were women. Many were crying.

Only when the light came up a little more, did I realise what had happened. Dieter, you fucking bastard! They'd stripped her naked, fucking naked, and hung her from the streetlamp, like a piece of cattle. Why the fuck did they do that? What did it achieve? What was her crime? She had just been nice to people. Okay, they were Americans, but for fuck's sake, she had just been decent. I felt myself welling up, as I glared at Dieter. He didn't look at me. Anton caught my glare. Tears were plain to see, running down my cheeks. He just looked down at his weapons. You bastards. I blinked rapidly to improve my vision. In the distance, someone reached up, trying to take her down. I caught a glimpse of something across her breasts. It was a crudely made sign, plain to see now; 'American Whore'. The whole thing was unreal. As if this whole situation wasn't bad enough, we had now resorted to killing our own, and for what? Would the locals fear us? Would they stop talking to the Americans? All I knew was we had sunk lower than I thought we could go. The Werewolves were deserters, insurgents, now murderers! I looked over at Gerhard. Streaks of tears also marked his cheeks. Was she of similar age to his daughter? I wasn't sure how old he was. For sure, he looked a lot older than me. But war could age a man, I supposed. In the distance, the locals fetched a ladder. An American soldier slowly climbed it to cut her down. I could still hear engines. All I knew was that the inevitable backlash from the Americans would be all the fiercer for the atrocity.

Maybe Dieter knew it too. He scrambled up the bank with one of the Panzerfaust that Thomas' team had in reserve, after the attack on the party in Schlangen. He stood proudly on the road, in plain view. "What the hell are you doing?" hissed Konrad. Dieter didn't answer. He put the Panzerfaust on his right shoulder, and operated the firing mechanism. The loud thud of the projectile launch caused my ears to ring. I followed the rocket, as it arced down the road. Most of the people at the streetlamp turned to face us, because of the sound of the launch.

The Panzerfaust skimmed off the road and exploded in front of them with a loud dull crump. The mass of people, including the citizens of Schlangen, slumped to the floor in a crumpled heap, the light-grey cloud of smoke and dust mixed with a red mist from their shattered bodies. Their screams and cries hit me. On the streetlamp, the girl's pale body swung wildly, pieces of it splintering off, as splinters carved through her. I was stunned to the point where I just couldn't take in what Dieter had done. I looked up at him, lost for words. He directed his menacing glare at me, his face full of an evil grin. "This is how we fight this fucking war!"

He then proceeded to drop the launcher, and took up his MP40, starting to squeeze single shots off down the road. Off to the right, brown-green figures began dashing between houses, into the gardens at the edge of the village. "Infantry!" roared Gerhard.

In a flash, we were all up on the road. I took aim with my MP40, also squeezing single shots off at bobbing brown-green figures, some of them now out in a field. I couldn't tell if I was hitting them, but I wasn't going to risk staying on the road to find out. I scrambled down, skirted right for about five metres, then found a better position on the bank. Rounds snapped over my head, some flicking off Bobby's broken panzer in a flurry of sparks. Gerhard moved off the road. But then he passed me, moving into the field, which I thought was madness, because he was closer to the enemy infantry. He hurled a grenade, which exploded in a light-grey cloud in the field. It seemed to subdue the enemy infantry we could see, but more appeared at distance on the road. "Infantry, centre!" roared Dieter. He was still standing defiantly on the road, rounds whizzing past him. Even the gravel near his feet was flicking up, due to bullet strikes. Was he mad?

I moved down the bank, sprinting to join Konrad. I noticed the girl's body swinging slightly on the streetlamp, being hit from both sides. Sweat stung my eyes, my heart pounding in my ears, making it hard to find targets. A blurred but prominent green mass appeared behind her. "Panzer!" I screamed. "Behind the girl's body!"

There was a loud thud to my left, blasting me in gravel. My ears and eyes began to sting. The tank must have fired. I sank down onto the bank, my head swimming, eyes raw. I tried to get grit out of my eyes. As my hearing returned, fire snapped over me. Dieter's bellow made me focus. "Get up here and fight, you little shit!" I looked up. He wasn't standing so proudly on the road anymore. He had adopted a lower, more life-preserving position, because the tank had made an appearance. "Yes you, you little shit, your Fuhrer commands it!" I nodded. Now was not the time to argue the merits of everything. I got to my knees, scanning the bank for a new position to fight. Konrad and Anton were now working as a pair, fighting for their lives, one moving whilst the other fired. "Gerhard!" roared Dieter, over a horrendous din of bullet snaps, just above his head. "The panzer is moving right, get ready!"

Gerhard came dashing down the line, grabbing two Panzerfaust that Anton and Konrad had left on the bank. "Erik," Gerhard commanded, "with me, let's go!" He scrambled away, me hard on his heels. We moved along the base of the bank, as quickly as we could. A new position offered cover. Bullets stopped snapping over our heads. The Americans were concentrating fire on our centre. He slowly moved up the bank, peering around. He shook his head. I could tell it was bad news. "We are going to have to cross the road to ensure a first-round hit." My heart sank. The bank was our only protection from enemy tanks and infantry. He snapped his fingers to signal the daring move. "Let's go!" He took off. Quickly, he was over the top, out of sight. I scrambled after him, praying the Americans wouldn't pick us off on the road.

A drainage ditch on the other side of the road was full of brambles. I fell into them face-first, causing me to wince. Gerhard was in no better position with them, but grinned at me nonetheless. We very quickly untangled ourselves from our thorny shackles, moving along the ditch on our hands and knees. It ran almost parallel with the foremost gardens and outhouses. I could hear Americans shouting over the din of the tank. I couldn't see the tank yet, but the ditch started vibrating, the vibration quickly increasing. Gerhard grabbed my arm. "Get that thing ready!" he said, giving me a Panzerfaust. "Keep low, do not let their infantry see you." I didn't need reminding of that requirement. I just nodded, carefully getting the Panzerfaust ready to fire, whilst laying on my front in the mud and wet. Readying the Panzerfaust was awkward, but I managed it. I carefully raised my profile with my arms, so I could peer over the lip of the ditch. The tank rattled into view. It was trying to creep around the side of a house, chewing up wire-strand fences, as it crushed its way through gardens. The tank's entire body was draped in sandbags, and short lengths of spare track. Up on the turret, a green and muddy crewmen was manning a huge machinegun. I was certain if he swivelled just a little, he would see us lying there, but he appeared more occupied with Dieter at our centre. Gerhard gave me a nudge. "Let it pass, then shoot it up the arse." Not what I wanted to hear, but it made sense. There was too much crap draped over the front of the tank, for a shot hitting it there to knock it out. The tank fired a shot from its main barrel. My ears burst into a high-pitched scream, my head thick and swimming. A huge geyser of gravel and bank shot up, somewhere close to Dieter's position. With a bit of luck, the Americans had killed the bastard. I was sure the tank commander was feeling rather confident, no infantry had followed him. Why would they? But I reflected that by continually moving position when alternating their fire, Konrad and Anton were, to their credit, making it look like we had more numbers. The tank rumbled and screeched, further forward towards the road, its backside slowly presenting itself to us, the firing angle gradually becoming more favourable. The machinegun crewman was really giving it some, the dull bass drumbeat almost constantly hammering Dieter's position. I hoped the machine-gunner was accurate. "Get ready!" ordered Gerhard. My stomach turned over as I moved to a semi-squatting position. The tank was creeping further away, its back end now fully exposed. "NOW!" Gerhard gasped. The loud thud of my launcher rendered me deaf again. There was a huge burst of sparks, dead centre on the backside of the tank. The impact knocked the machine-gunner off his aim. He sprawled over his gun. Heavy black smoke began pouring out of the back decks. The engine coughed, then spluttered out of action. The lumbering beast rolled to a stop. Gerhard grabbed my arm. "Let's go!" he shouted.

I ditched the launcher, sprinting after him, straight into the mire of brambles, which pierced and scratched at our skin and uniforms. Behind me, I heard the squeak and heavy clatter of turret hatches. I glanced back. The tank crew, some smouldering, were scrabbling out of their stricken vehicle. They were more concerned with rolling around on the grass, putting out their smouldering clothing, than dealing with us. We got free of the brambles, but our entire world became the focus of the enemy's fury. Mud, grass and gravel flicked up around us, amid a horrendous din of snaps and whizzes. We scrambled like maniacs across the road on our hands and knees, to the relative safety of the bank on the other side. Soaked with sweat, breathing like it was our last, we rolled down to the base of the bank. It had been fucking close. "We can't stay here, let's move!" ordered Gerhard, clambering to his feet. He set off at a crouch, back towards our two stricken panzers on the bank. I stumbled to my feet and followed him.

When we got back to our panzers, I was disappointed. Dieter was still alive, in cover at the base of the bank. He was wounded, a large long gash along the side of his face, blood very fresh. Anton and Konrad weren't dashing about like maniacs. They were beside him, checking their magazines. The snaps coming over the top of us were constant now, mud and gravel occasionally flicking up. Dieter grinned, offering me his hand. "Good kill there, boy, nice shooting!" I just looked at his hand, staring back at him. I was in no mood to be associated with an arsehole. His devilish grin disappeared. He glanced at Gerhard, who glared at him. Dieter nodded, almost a sign of capitulation. "Are we ready to go?"

'Ready!' Anton and Konrad barked in response.

Dieter nodded again. "Get your grenades ready. On my order, we throw them straight down the street, clear?" We all just wanted to get the fuck out of there. Grenades at the ready, Dieter led our crawl to the top of the bank. He held out his right arm at shoulder level. "Get ready… NOW!"

I hurled my grenade so hard, I thought I had injured myself. Our grenades arced almost effortlessly towards the pile of dead and wounded at the streetlamp. Some other people had come out to the aid of the wounded, but scrambled out of the way of our grenades, which bounced and settled around the pile. Above, the hanging girl was now just a pale and bloody carcass, like one you might see in a butcher's window. As the grenades exploded, shreds of bone, muscle and clothing flicked all over the street. Her noose cut by grenade splinters, the hanging girl fell, slamming face-first onto the bloody, cobbled street. A loud thud to our right stunned me, causing my right side to throb, and my right ear to ring. Who was shooting at us?

"FOLLOW ME!" roared Dieter. He took off down the road, towards the streetlamp. Before I could even comprehend his madness, Konrad and Anton were running after him, firing as they went, roaring at the top of their voices.

Gerhard didn't follow. Why? Perhaps he wasn't entertaining the madness anymore. "Down here, boy." Spinning around, I saw him lying at the bottom of the bank, a bloody hand clasping his chest, his other hand still clasping his weapon. Blood was running from his mouth and nostrils. I slid down the bank to tend to my old friend. "I got hit as I threw my grenade," he managed between blood-spraying coughs, his lips smeared. 'I only just managed to get it clear of us." The recent explosion to my right had been his grenade. I began welling up, as I tried to pull his hand away to inspect his wound. He kept his hand firmly in place. Despite being gravely wounded, he was still strong as an ox. "Leave it, boy. It's okay." Down the road, all hell had broken loose, the weight of fire horrendous. The Americans were giving our three men in the open their undivided attention. Why did our guys stupidly run down the road? Hadn't enough people died today? Gerhard placed a hand on my elbow. "You must go now, Erik. Get back to the roadblock. You don't have to be here anymore."

I wiped my tears with my torn muddy sleeve. "What about you?"

"I've had my war, Erik. You need to go and have yours, please." He coughed up more blood. "Go boy. The Americans will not spare you, please go now." The sound of fire started to peter away. The Americans would be advancing up the road soon. "Go Erik, get away from here. You are just a boy. Don't waste your life, by looking after an old fool like me." He shoved his weapon at me, and gave me a slap around the ear. "Go now!" He looked such a sorry broken mess. He nodded, and waved me away. I was beside myself, having to abandon a friend to the enemy. I ran away along the base of the bank, just as I had after the artillery assault. Once more, this same position had destroyed friendships I had forged in this awful fucking mess. What have you got yourself into here, Erik?

Chapter Fourteen – Rearguard Action

I paused for breath, diving into a ditch, some way towards the roadblock. I slumped on my back, wiping tear streaks from my face. I truly was in a world of shit. I just wished it would all be over soon. I didn't have a clue how I was going to make it home. If I surrendered, the Americans would probably shoot me out of hand, or even worse, hand me over to the Russians. Max's warning remained with me. No one was taking SS prisoners, no one. For sure, we were going to pay dearly for this war.

I could just make out our destroyed panzers and halftrack, before the entrance to Schlangen. A column of thick black smoke marked the tank I had knocked out. I caught a glimpse of flame licking the scorched shell of the vehicle. Now and again, loud pops signalled what may have been its ammunition cooking off, sparks erupting from it. There was lots of movement in the area of the streetlamp; the shimmering profile of soldiers, and what looked like armour. The Americans were coming. I sought the relative sanctuary of the woods, just off the road, the roar of tank engines echoing, as I began stumbling through the trees.

An armoured vehicle began to approach. Troops jumped off the back. A tank fired its main gun into the woods. The echo was horrendous, making me jump as I stumbled on. A long burst of machinegun fire followed, red tracer punching deep into the wood line, flicking off in random directions. A further series of loud snaps had me making my way to a ditch, where I laid belly down. More tank rounds thundered past, deep into darker woodland. A hornets' nest of tracer began, snapping all over the place, gravel and mud flicking all around me. The Americans were taking no chances, thinking there were lots of us; searching fire to pick off multiple unseen targets. A loud roar of horsepower could only have been the armoured vehicle advancing further. Infantry from it had to be pushing forward. My stomach turned. I knew I couldn't stay where I was. I scrambled away along the ditch, trying to distance myself from them. Before long, I was coated in mud, trying to keep as low as possible, trying to make good speed, as more tank rounds thundered above. Almighty echoes of explosions accompanied loud sharp cracks, as trees got smashed. Some trees crashed to earth with their canopies. One nearby tree received a direct hit; pale timber splinters showering me, sticking to the mire I was covered in. If I had to fight now, my weapon would fail, as it too was coated. On the Senne, Max would have kicked my arse for allowing it to dirty up.

The firing gradually reduced; just the odd thunder of tank shells, and the odd ripple of machinegun fire. Maybe turning the Teutoburger Wald into matchwood had taken up too much of their ammunition, but that suited me fine. What wasn't going away was the constant throb of tank engines, the metallic squeal of tracks. Were they slowly following me down the road, humouring me, waiting for me to get tired and give up? I dared not look back, and just kept scrambling forward. Just short of what for some reason seemed to be more familiar surroundings, I had to stop. My hands were a muddy mess of splinters and cuts. I knew I looked a sorry state, and didn't give a shit about it. But I was steaming in the chilled air, my breathing also too prominent. I just hoped their gunners were more interested in breakfast now. The firing stopped altogether, which was a relief.

Two tanks appeared on the road, side-by-side. Their turret crews began talking to each other. Two guys pored over a map, another two lighting cigarettes. Through the shimmer of exhaust fumes, I saw infantry crossing the road, moving into the forest, towards me. The roadblock had to be just up ahead; I knew I was somewhere close to the false horizon. I knew I couldn't enjoy the view anymore, I needed to warn Thomas and his guys.

I remained in the ditch for a while, before moving back into the woods, breaking into a jog. I couldn't see the roadblock, maybe because of the effort we put into its construction. With a bit of luck, their turret crews wouldn't see it 'til the last possible moment. I moved into a ditch, and after a while, I spotted some trees lying across the road. I began to carefully pick my way through the woods again, making my way towards the trees forming the roadblock.

I heard a strange groaning, and what could only be described as sobbing. I stood still, trying to focus on where it was coming from. Animal? Possibly livestock? I started to walk towards the sounds. Apart from the groaning and sobbing, I only heard creaking branches above me. I heard what might have been a cough, followed by a loud groan. It was coming from above. A construction of logs suddenly appeared before me, extending upwards. Oh my fucking God! Whatever food remained in my stomach fought its way into my mouth. I made a vain attempt to hold it down, but it burnt my nostrils, as it found another way out. I collapsed to my hands and knees, retching my life away in stomach-ripping spasms. Once I managed to get it under control, I cuffed away string-like vomit from my lips. But I had to look again.

It was the American prisoner from Schlangen, naked as the day he was born, dried blood all over his face and chest. Both his ears were a clotted mass of blood. His ankles were pinned with one of our metal pickets, which had clearly been smashed through with some force, blood clotting below. His feet and ankles were bloated black and purple, looking fit to burst. Further up, his hands looked no better, spread palms uppermost, a picket hammered through each one. He groaned, gargled, spluttering blood, sobbing. I stood up. I carefully made my way around to his left. He yelped as I stood on a log. I apologised under my breath, vibration causing him discomfort. I gingerly placed my feet further from his. I avoided any contact with a log running behind his shoulders. His hands were skewered, close to either end of it. He appeared to struggle to hold his head still. I made to investigate why, but his sudden outburst jolted me, almost causing me to fall. "Nooooo!" he gargled. "Gren-ade, gren-ade!"

"Don't touch him!" a voice commanded. I snapped my head left. Thomas was standing on a log, an MP40 in his hands. A sneering, menacing leer covered his face; full of wickedness, void of any compassion.

"Gren-ade?" I enquired.

Thomas' leer became a grin. "Look under his head." I put my cheek to the log behind the American's shoulders. A grenade of some description was pinned behind his head. I couldn't confirm the grenade's design, since it was caked in dry blood, and partly covered by his hair. Obviously, if he moved his head too much, the grenade would detonate. "Took it from the bastards who ambushed us in the gardens," confirmed Thomas. "You must have heard it." I did recall hearing a commotion behind the dark alleyway in Schlangen, as Dieter led us away from the rocket attack on the party. We had found two Americans in the gardens. I nodded at Thomas. I was too tired and afraid to question him on the atrocity inflicted on the prisoner. I wasn't quite sure who I feared most, the Americans or my own side. We had clearly entered the darkest realms of the surreal. Desperate spiteful measures by desperate spiteful men. "Where are Dieter and the others?" Thomas enquired.

"He hung the girl, for the Americans and locals to find her." I tried to establish whether there was so much as a glimmer of humanity left in Thomas. His face remained unmoved.

"And?" he pressed.

"Dieter ambushed a group, who were trying to cut her down. He killed both the enemy and locals."

His menacing leer returned. "Go on!"

"We got into a fight with infantry and armour. Gerhard and I knocked out a panzer and some infantry, but there was just too much to keep at bay. We threw grenades. Dieter, Anton and Konrad charged the enemy. I remained with Gerhard, who was badly wounded."

His expression showed a flicker of humanity. "Is Gerhard dead?"

"I don't know. He told me to get back here and warn you."

"Warn us? About what?"

"They have panzers and infantry, just along the road. They were firing into the woods."

His demeanour changed; less demonic, more professional. "Show me!"

The American gargled and sobbed as we left him. I led Thomas towards the road. "Just as the road goes out of sight, there are at least two panzers. Infantry were moving into the woods on this side. I don't know about the other side, though."

He scanned around with binoculars, then nodded. "Good boy, come with me."

Before long, we were behind the roadblock. The remainder of the guys were there, including Dennis and Otto, who had MG-42s. Draped in belt ammunition, they were ready to fight. Thomas called a huddle. "The boy has just returned from Schlangen. Dieter killed the girl. He also killed the rest of his team, trying to be a fucking hero." Some of the guys glanced at each other, slowly shaking their heads. Was it compassion for the poor girl, or for the guys we had lost? Who knew anymore? "Erik informs me that the Americans are moving up here with panzers and infantry. At this time, we know there are infantry in the woods, on the side we just came in from. There are at least two panzers on the road." He pointed at Lars. "Move forward on the other side of the road. See if there are any infantry over there, then get back to me quickly, so I can site you all effectively." Lars nodded, and moved away. "We have limited resources," continued Thomas. "We must hit them hard, and then withdraw. If we can break clean, we will fall back to the house. If we become separated, and the enemy are on your tail, stay away from the house, do you understand?"

We all nodded. I started to shiver and sweat with nerves again. Did you ever lose them? A dreadful, gargling cough emanated from our prisoner, crucified on the logs. "What about him?" Viktor enquired.

Thomas grinned. "He stays there. The lead tank will have a nice surprise." Felix chuckled into his sleeve, his face full of wickedness.

I felt a nudge. Johann grinned at me. "You okay?"

I just nodded. Where would it all end? I heard heavy laboured breathing. Lars re-joined us, and took a moment to get his breath back. "No infantry on the other side of the road. Two panzers up front, staggered. Infantry ahead on this side." He gasped.

"Panzerfaust on this side," Thomas said urgently, "MGs on the other. We hit the panzers first. Machine-gunners, kill as many infantry as you can, but your main job is to prevent them getting over the road, understood? We don't want to be caught in crossfire." We all nodded. The group began to scatter. "Erik, follow Otto," added Thomas, "help him with his MG-42."

I nodded. I made my way into the woods, trying to identify the fighting positions we had prepared. I heard a click of fingers. Otto waved me over. Just short of his position, I got down on my belly, not wanting to give our position away to a steely-eyed enemy soldier. I crawled into the small construction of mud-smeared logs. "Right, boy," he commanded, "stay on my left side, and help with the ammunition." I ensured the belt ammunition was the right way around, ready to feed into the gun. He adjusted the sights for the current conditions; minimum range, close fighting. He placed his stick grenades down. "When I say so, throw one out to our front. I don't want their infantry coming in on top of us, okay?" I couldn't agree more. That would be very bad. Our side of the ambush was simple. We wouldn't open fire until the rockets hit the tanks. With the tanks taken care of, we stood a better chance of taking on their infantry. All in all, we had about a thousand rounds for our gun. It was probably the same for Dennis. Short controlled bursts would be needed to make the ammo last. The throbbing of tank engines began to echo. Now it was just a waiting game. The thing that would test our nerve was staying quiet, until the tanks were at the logs. If their infantry were leading, they might even pass around the roadblock without seeing us. I wasn't a tactician, but I would have my infantry forward, in order to detect or spring any tank trap. But I hoped their infantry wouldn't be leading. Hitting the tanks, whilst infantry were behind us, would not be a good prospect.

The engine noise grew louder. I heard the squeal of tracks. I peered through a small gap between the logs. On my stomach, I could see very little. But on the slope leading up to the false horizon, I soon made out the light-grey plumes of tank exhaust. I concluded that overgrown ferns were preventing me from seeing any infantry. Their infantry could have been right in front of us, for all I knew. Otto gave me a gentle nudge. "Two panzers," he mouthed. "Thirty plus infantry." I felt nauseous. Two MG-42s against a large platoon. If we knocked out the tanks, we stood a fighting chance.

The approaching engine pitch changed, indicating the armour was approaching the roadblock. My hands were sweaty, my heart pounding in my ears, something that always seemed to happen, just before all hell broke loose. I peered down at my MP40. It was still coated in mud. I cursed myself for not at least checking it would still work. You fool, Erik! "The infantry is leading," mouthed Otto. He nodded at the grenades. "Get ready," he mouthed again. I took hold of one of them, my hands visibly shaking. I tried to prepare it, but I was losing the battle with the shakes. Otto gently placed his left hand on mine, and gave me a wink. He slowly drew his hand away, and I found I was no longer shaking. He knew I was scared, and knew now was not the time to mock me. He needed me ready to fight, so his fatherly gesture went a long way. I was ready now. All I needed to do was arm the grenade and throw it.

The roar of the engines increased to a terrifying climax. Over the roar, the Americans couldn't possibly hear the screams and shouts of their crucified colleague, and almost certainly hadn't seen him yet. I peered out, and saw the cluttered, muddy green profile of the tank, climbing off the road in our direction. It skirted round, moving towards our prisoner. A scream went right through me. The engine gave out an almighty roar, as the turret lifted. The tank crew were down in their fighting positions, not exposed. Maybe their periscopes wouldn't allow them to see the crucified man.

I heard foreign voices, close to our position. They began shouting, hollering and whistling, maybe to get the attention of the tank. A dull thud echoed over the engine noise. The crucified American had detonated all over the front of the tank, red strands intertwined with wood bark and timber splinters, his struggle with the grenade at an end. Maybe the tank's arrival had caused his final demise.

Suddenly, the tank was overwhelmed by bright showers of sparks, as our rockets found their mark. The detonations almost instantly dulled, as steel was penetrated. Otto's MG-42 burst into life in short, sharp rippling bursts. "Throw the fucking grenade!" he barked, without even looking at me. I knelt up to see their infantry in spades. Many began running about, the odd muzzle flash giving away those not moving. A few were cut down by Dennis' MG-42. I threw the grenade towards what looked like a cluster of infantry, before ducking back into cover. I didn't see where the grenade landed, but made out its dull thud over the deafening chatter of Otto's bursts. The odd snap of incoming passed overhead, along with the splintering crunch of their rounds hitting our cover. I heard an outrageous roar of engine and transmission, but couldn't identify the vehicle. I busied myself, making sure there was enough slack in the MG-42's ammunition belt to prevent a stoppage. The tank hit by our rockets became a column of pitch-black smoke, its crew trying to bail out. Some bundled out towards us, but Dennis had an angle to take care of them, his bursts shattering them, easy pickings. They slumped into a dull green, wet and muddy pile. Less troops to fight.

The incoming infantry became sporadic at best. Our careful preparation of the roadblock and surrounding area had paid off. Their infantry began to give ground, most leaving wounded where they fell. Those making heroic attempts to recover their wounded comrades were ruthlessly cut down by our MG-42s. The loud bass drumbeat of a heavy machinegun entered the fray. I had no idea where it was. Perhaps it was the second tank, engaging the rocket teams. "Panzer in the woods!" roared Otto at the top of his voice, scaring the shit out of me. I carefully peered out. The second tank had pushed into the woods to support their infantry. But it was being held at bay by some of the logs we had arranged, and a tree stump that remained from our activity. The tank's heavy machinegun had a good angle on Dennis' position, slowly disintegrating his cover with heavy bursts. Dennis and Johann were no longer fighting, but merely cowering. Otto fired bursts, trying to deal with the troublesome enemy gunner, but he just couldn't get the angle. "Get them rocket arseholes over here, or we are fucked!" he roared.

I prepared to make a suicide dash towards Dennis. But Felix must have heard Otto, since he was crawling like a mad man, two Panzerfaust across his forearms. I waved Felix into our cover. He was gasping for breath, sweating like mad. "We killed the first panzer, damaged the second!" he gasped.

Otto didn't even look at him. "Well, go kill the fucker, or we are in trouble!"

I looked at Felix, who merely rolled his eyes, and prepared one of the rockets. He handed me his MP40. "Come with me, I'm going to need protection." He wasn't serious, surely. But I dared not refuse. I checked to ensure there was a round in the chamber of his MP40, and gave him a nod. He flipped onto his stomach, and crawled down to the roadside ditch. I crawled like a maniac to join him. So far, so good. We needed to move another 30 metres or so, to find a good firing position. We needed to be quick, because Dennis and Johann were in trouble, their cover now nothing more than splintered timber. Felix took off at a fast pace, breathing so heavily, I was scared it would give us away. Still in the ditch, we had to literally clamber over shot-up crew from the destroyed tank. My stomach turned over; they were still warm, still bleeding out. One was still groaning. Otto's consistently short bursts reassured me of covering fire, but it felt like the longest 30 metres of my life. We got there, the tank nose-in to the woods, a short distance away. Its right side was already badly scored and chipped, smouldering equipment hanging on the side from our first strike. The gunner up on the turret was too engrossed with Dennis and Johann to notice us. I pushed myself against a wall of the ditch, so back blast from Felix's launcher wouldn't take my head off. Felix sprung to a kneeling position and fired. The loud thud of the launching projectile once again turned my battle soundtrack into a long constant ring. I felt the thud of impact as the rocket hit the tank, slap bang in the side. A huge flurry of sparks showered the immediate area. I was already on my belly, crawling back along the ditch like a man possessed, having already experienced the enemy's fury towards anti-tank teams. Once I made it past the shot-up enemies in the ditch, I looked back. My heart sank. Felix was still in the position from where he fired the rocket, minus his head; still in the kneeling position, slumped against a side of the ditch. His blood had turned his filthy tunic black. The smoking launch tube laid across his thigh. He had done his job, however. The tank was smouldering pitch-black smoke from its engine decks. As my hearing improved, I heard the rippling bursts from both Dennis and Otto's MG42-s, as they destroyed the emerging tank crew, no quarter given.

The American infantry lost the stomach to continue. They slowly moved back, firing as they went. Their fire wasn't landing anywhere near us, the odd snap splintering the canopy above. Before long, there was no more gunfire, just the crackling, popping and fizzing of the two burning tanks, one of which still had its engine running. I began to pick up the groaning of American wounded. "Friendlies coming in!" a voice behind me shouted. Thomas led Lars and Viktor to me. They kept their weapons close at hand, as they slumped just behind me. Otto, Dennis and Johann joined us from their positions, carrying smouldering MG-42s by their carrying handles. Dennis' MG-42 was almost out of ammunition. He and Johann looked rather worse for wear, which was understandable. Some of the guys coughed and spluttered, others rolling cigarettes. I could still hear enemy wounded groaning, and the sounds of burning tanks, but other than that, all was rather tranquil again.

There was no chat whilst we rested. The adrenalin had gone, for now at least. The aroma of tobacco gave me a lovely feeling of warmth. Again, I was almost in envy of those who smoked. By choice alone, I had denied myself one of the last pastimes you could call your own. Smoking; such a simple pleasure, during dark times such as now. "We need to finish here," stated Thomas, "and get back to the house. I don't think we will see the Americans, anymore today." There were nods around me. The smokers enjoyed a last drag on their cigarettes. We slowly got to our feet, and got our gear together. Our loads were now considerably lighter, since we had used almost all of our belt ammunition. We had but a couple of Panzerfaust left between us, but there were more at the house. I had never thought to ask how they managed to obtain such a vast amount of ammunition and weaponry. I think at this stage of the war, scrounging was the name of the game for the German army. I collected up the remaining grenades, stuffing them into my belt. Otto picked up his MG-42, with its small amount of remaining belt ammunition. My sorry-looking MP40 would have to be cleaned immediately, once we were back at the house.

Just as Lars began to lead off, Thomas put his hand on my shoulder. "There is one more thing we need to do. I need your help."

I nodded, peering around at the others. Their evil grins had returned. My stomach tightened. "Have I done something wrong?" I quietly asked.

With a smile, Thomas shook his head. "Good God, no Erik. You have fought bravely today. We just need to sort out Felix. That is all. Not an easy task, but it must be done."

I nodded. Fair enough. Not ideal, but there it was. Lars led the others away. I followed Thomas towards Felix. Sometimes, you get used to fighting at a particular location, but afterwards, you sometimes see it from a totally different perspective. Their infantry had plenty of cover to exploit near the roadblock. They could have outflanked us through the woods. But maybe the Americans really did fear the forests. We stood next to what was left of Felix. I could just make out the top of his spine, protruding from his black torso, which was shattered and shredded by gunfire. Half his face was lying on his shoulder, like an empty rubber mask. My stomach churned. Only the wall of the ditch had kept him propped up. His propped-up body had just served as a flash target for more enemy fire. Truly grim. Anything of value probably couldn't be recovered from him. The immediate area was littered with enemy dead and wounded. It was over for the dead. As for the wounded, they could only look forward to a long, slow cold night in a German forest. Thomas walked slowly amongst the dead and dying. The groans and fidgeting of the wounded gave them away. One attempted to get onto his hands and knees. He slowly pushed himself up, as Thomas stood next to him. Thomas moved slowly round, until he was facing the head of the wounded American, who mustered all his strength to look up. The American mumbled something under his breath, which I couldn't understand. Thomas glared at him, slowly drawing his Luger pistol from its holster. My stomach flipped immediately, the real nature of my task with Thomas becoming apparent. His face full of hate, Thomas pointed his pistol at the American's face. "Heil Hitler!" The American's face collapsed with the sheer energy of the bullet, which blew out the back of his skull. His shattered head, still attached at the neck, thudded to the ground. His torso and legs remained in a kneeling position, his backside in the air.

Thomas' shot had made me jump, but hadn't shocked me. We had new rules around here. That was plain to see. But I was determined not to fall foul of the rules. I wanted to live. I was certainly more scared of my own countrymen than the enemy. I just stared at the American's body, empty of emotion. Thomas caught my gaze. "Erik, show no mercy." He offered me the pistol grip of the Luger. I was shocked by his order. I was to be his executioner. If I refused, it could well be me, lying next to the American. I took the pistol from Thomas, its grip still warm. My use of pistols had been minimal at best. We hadn't really got into pistol shooting on the Senne; basic instruction, not much else. It was more of a weapon for panzer crews and officers. But after Thomas' initial shot, I knew there would be a fresh round in the breech. I looked around for my first American victim. A blood-curdling cough gave one away. I slowly made my way over. He was lying face down, helmet still on, torso moving as he breathed heavily. How was I to turn him over? What if he grabbed me? I looked at Thomas, who just glared at me, almost daring me to refuse. If I just put the muzzle under the rim of the enemy's helmet, it would do the job. I bent over, my shaking hand causing the barrel to rattle against the rim. I could hear my victim sobbing. He knew it was his time. Executed by a child, of all things. I looked at Thomas again. His arms were crossed, his face full of a wicked leer. He nodded his approval. I pulled the trigger. The enemy's head shattered instantly, as the pistol snapped back in my hand. I stood up. My boots were speckled with my victim's blood. Thomas walked towards me, hand outstretched. I handed him the pistol. He patted me on the shoulder. "Go behind the roadblock. Wait for me there." I nodded. Numb was the best way to describe how I felt. I was pretty certain I had taken lives, but to kill someone up close was a whole new experience. I slowly made my way to the roadblock, flinching every time I heard a shot, echoing loudly through the trees. Thomas was taking his time, clearly enjoying his work. Before long, there were no more shots. He soon appeared beside me. "Let's get out of here. I'm hungry, and ready for coffee." But food was the furthest thing from my mind at that moment, despite the fact I couldn't remember the last time I had eaten.

Chapter Fifteen – The Pied Piper

I trudged down the road to Berlebeck with Thomas. I couldn't think of anything to talk about. My energy was starting to drain. The ambush of the party in Schlangen felt like a lifetime ago. The girl. Her image came to the front of my mind. Why did we have to kill the girl? Killing the enemy, wounded or otherwise, was something I could stomach better, than murdering a girl who was just trying to be hospitable in such a shit situation. Were we at a time where we could literally get away with murder? Did the war throw all of society's rules out the window? What have you got yourself into here, Erik?

Johann greeted us at the house. All the blackout curtains were in place. It was just starting to turn dusk, the days still short and cold. Thomas ordered him to stand watch inside the house. The idea was that if enemy scouts spotted a lone sentry, it usually meant he was guarding a position.

I was later tasked with helping Johann to arrange a room upstairs, making it a watchtower of sorts. With no light in the room, we hung just one sheet of blackout material in the window frame, so we could peer through the window. If enemies entered the town, it would be easy to creep down to the basement, warning everyone for action.

Johann had first watch. Everyone else gathered in the kitchen. Coffee was doing the rounds. Viktor had some potato and vegetable mix going on the stove. The conversation was rather subdued, mainly due to our lack of numbers. There were now enough seats at the table for everyone. Thomas sat at the end. Large chunks of bread, almost stiff with staleness now, were in everyone's hands. No one was really fussy. I just felt hungry. We ate in silence. I was tired, everyone was tired. Only Viktor stayed on his feet, tending the boiling pot. I made short work of my bread, but took my time over the coffee. With both hands cupped around the metal mug, I felt at peace; relaxed, almost sedate. The rising warmth of the house was making me drowsy. We didn't have a fire going, since that could give us away, but just being indoors felt very cosy. I hoped to get some sleep very soon, since for sure, I needed it. My weapons would need cleaning first, I couldn't neglect them anymore. "We need to prepare to relocate," Thomas said, "back towards Detmold." Detmold wasn't too far away, just six kilometres to the north. "That roadblock has served its purpose. No point wasting lives there now. If I was a betting man, they will crucify it with artillery tomorrow, before they venture back up there." My thoughts turned to the crucified American. Had the tank crew heading in his direction even known he was there? "The Americans will be in Berlebeck soon," Thomas stated, "mark my words. All we can do is play for time and punish them, when and where we can."

Some of the guys made their way to the cellar. I was instructed to relieve Johann, so he could eat. I was so tired, I didn't have the strength or courage to protest. I quickly shuffled into the cellar to grab some rags and weapon oil, so I could tend to my filthy MP40, whilst in the watchtower. I took all my fighting gear with me, should the Americans be rude enough to turn up, whilst I was up there. Ravenous and thirsty, Johann was very grateful to be relieved. I began to peer out into the garden. I chose to remain standing whilst I cleaned my MP40, the temptation to sit would only result in me falling asleep. Even standing, if I closed my eyes for a second, only the shock of my buckling knees kept me awake.

Boots thudded up the stairs. Lars stood in the doorway. Was my duty over already? He was full of smiles, armed with his weapons, a pot of coffee and two mugs. "Thought you could do with some company, and some of this stuff to keep you awake." He offered me an empty cup.

"Thank you, I am shattered!" I croaked.

He nodded. "I know how you feel, I'm ready for bed. But through the night, we need two people on at any one time." He put the pot and his cup on a bedside dresser, then emptied the drawers, neatly stacking their contents in a corner. He carefully slid the dresser to the centre of the room, putting the pot and coffee cup on it, before arranging his weapons below the window frame. "I'm not one for wrecking people's property." He beamed. "I would be very pissed off, if any of our soldiers trashed my house." Such rare compassion in these times of madness. He poured us both coffee, and invited me to sit on the dresser with him. It was relatively comfortable, and we had a good view of the gardens. Why hadn't I thought of it? The enjoyable strong coffee took the edge off my tiredness. A comfortable but awkward silence hung for a while. "So, young Erik," he eventually said. "After the war, will you stay in the SS?"

I wasn't too sure how to deal with the question, without sounding out of turn. "Well, that depends."

He took a sip of coffee. "On what?"

I was nervous about the subject, but had put myself in a fucking corner already. I swallowed hard. "If we win."

He looked down at his cup. Was he testing my loyalty? Had I already failed? Was I now one of many defeatists, riddling our shattered nation? "What makes you think we are losing?" he pushed. I wished I was on duty by myself. I could see the conversation going bad. He looked sternly at me. "Well?"

I took a deep breath. "May I speak freely?" He slowly nodded. "The Russians are very close to Berlin," I began. "We happen to be fighting the Americans. I don't know where the

British and Canadians are. We hung a girl yesterday, because she was talking to the Americans. We crucified a prisoner at the roadblock, and I'm not sure if we are on a winning streak right now. Everything is getting more spiteful, more wicked. I fought the Americans at Kirchborchen, not too long ago, and that felt more like, shall we say, a fair fight." I knew I had said too much. It was time for me to shut the fuck up.

His demeanour relaxed. He nodded again. "You are a bright kid, Erik, I'll give you that. Desperate times call for desperate measures. More coffee?"

Coffee? I felt I was about to be shot for being defeatist. "Am I in trouble?"

He looked at me with a puzzled expression. "For what? Knowing when the chips are down? Erik, I'm too long in the tooth, to really give a damn about the misgivings of the German people. I just won't allow the invaders to relax, and enjoy the spoils of our country. You are just a boy, enjoy being just that. There are too many men fucking this whole situation up, regardless of their reservations." He broke into a friendly grin. "Enjoy the war, Erik, that's all that matters right now." I thought of Bobby. He just wanted to survive the war and go home. I wanted to go home. Lars told me that he was from Dortmund, a huge industrial city. He thought it would fall into American hands, not knowing if his family were safe. He lived for the fight. Right now, it was his life.

He wasn't interested in surrendering. The Americans hated the SS. It was no secret. He had escaped from the Ardennes with his life and his clothes, his unit chewed up by the sheer weight of American firepower. So for sure, he had an axe to grind with them.

It was dark again, before he asked me to go to the cellar, and give Otto and Viktor a shove for their turn on sentry duty. I gathered up all my equipment, and made my way downstairs. I tried to be as quiet as possible. In the soft light of oil lamps in the cellar, I made out Thomas' profile at the radio set. A speaker crackled, a very grainy voice giving instructions on how to use a Panzerfaust. What type of radio station was it? It certainly wasn't Lili Marlene. "Who is that broadcasting?" I whispered.

"The Reich Minister. Radio Werewolf. It now calls for the German nation to rise up, and fight the invaders. Demanding that every man, woman and child take up arms, and defend the Reich. And to destroy those who collaborate with the enemy. Throughout the broadcast, everyone receives instructions on how to use certain weapons." There had to be millions of weapons, strewn all over the country for civilians to use. So we were losing. Why else would citizens have to fight? The end of the war had to be near. "Aren't you supposed to be waking up your relief, Erik?"

"Er, yes, sorry to pester you," I stammered.

He gave me a warm smile. "You need to rest, boy. You've had some crazy adventures recently." I nodded as I backed away. I felt like a persistent child, that didn't know when to be quiet. There were a lot of empty cot beds. I tried to find Otto and Viktor in the dull glow. Desperately needing sleep, I gently nudged them both, impatiently waiting for them to rise. They rose noisily. Others threatened them with slow and violent deaths, if they didn't stay quiet; the usual banter of a barracks, nothing ever changes. Viktor and Otto looked exhausted, as they clumsily stumbled upstairs with their weapons, but it was their turn on sentry duty. I found myself an empty cot. I think it was Gerhard's. I missed that man. He was a nice guy. I had liked him. I didn't know too much about his exploits during the war, nor did I really care. As I lay down, the heavy steps of Lars thudded and creaked down the steps. He stopped to chat to Thomas. I fretted Lars would tell him about our conversation upstairs, but I relaxed slightly when they chuckled in light amusement, perhaps at Otto and Viktor's expense. I put the full weight of my head onto a makeshift pillow. The last thing I heard was someone teaching the nation how to use an MG-42.

There were heavy boots on the floor above. Heavy boots on creaking steps. Raised angry voices. Furniture being tossed aside.

My world exploded to life, as I crashed face-first to the hard stone floor. Had I fallen out of bed? I turned onto my back, and as my world came into focus, my heart jumped into my throat. Above me stood Dieter; filthy, bloodied and angry. "You weak, spineless little shit," he snarled. Before I could say anything, he dragged me up by my shirt and groin, shoving me heavily against a wall. All the wind was knocked out of me. I was seeing sparkles, as I fought to fill my lungs with air. I wasn't dreaming. He was very much real. So was the burning sensation in my stomach, due to being lifted by my balls.

"What's going on here?" Thomas demanded, over the commotion of others gathering round.

"This little shit deserted us in the face of the enemy," snarled Dieter through gritted teeth. "He ran away!" he roared, throwing me to the floor. I landed heavily on my left side, winded again. I curled up, expecting the angry giant to put the boot in.

It never came. Thomas stepped forward in front of Dieter, who was glaring down at me. "Is this true?" Thomas barked. "Did you run away from battle?"

I looked up, trying to draw breath. Now both their faces were full of anger. Dieter went for me again, but Thomas held him off. "Let him speak!" said Thomas. I always thought Dieter was the leader.

"Dieter charged the enemy," I forced out, "whilst I tended to Gerhard, who was wounded. Anton and Konrad followed Dieter into the attack. Gerhard was in a bad way."

They looked no less angry. Thomas took a sudden step forward, which made me flinch. He squatted down, looking me straight in the eyes. "Listen to me, boy," his tone soft but stern. "In the heat of battle, you leave the wounded where they fall, do you understand?"

"Yes sir!" I responded, trying not to well up.

He nodded slowly, rising to his feet. He addressed everyone, but looked at Dieter. "The boy will not let any of us down again. He tended to a wounded comrade. He is not hardened to our expectations, as of yet. Hopefully, my one-to-one class yesterday purged some of his youthful weakness from him." He looked down at me, summoning me up. I clambered to my feet, wiping tears from my filthy face. Everyone nodded, some beginning to go about their business. Thomas firmly gripped my shoulder, before making his way back to the radio set. I was very quickly left alone with Dieter. He gave me a rough shove against the wall, but I was ready for it, so wasn't winded.

But as he turned to walk away, a phrase roared from upstairs, one I never wanted to hear at the house. 'American infantry!' The house suddenly vibrated with the familiar rippling bursts of MG-42. Those who had gone back to their cots sprung up, like they had just received an electric shock. Many frantically scrambled for boots and weapons. Those dressed quickly stampeded up the steps. A huge thud rocked the house, causing dust and timber splinters to rain down on us. Those caught on the steps came crashing down on top of each other.

'Panzerschreck!' came a roar from upstairs. The Americans had their own version of bazooka. Another rocket hit the house, just as the guys in a pile at the bottom of the steps untangled themselves. The second thud was louder, my ears ringing. I now had my boots on, my weapons in my hands. I saw Thomas stood at the radio table, pointing his MP40 at Dieter, who was moving away towards the steps. "You are a fucking arsehole!" Thomas roared at him, over a dreadful din of gunfire and shouting from the kitchen. "You led the rats here, like an American Pied Piper!"

Dieter did not contest the allegation, instead barging his way up the steps. Thomas' glare then fixed on me. I dared not move. Maybe Thomas and I had led the Americans to the house, and they allowed Dieter through unmolested. Thomas flicked his head to the steps. I quickly complied, staggering upwards, crawling into the kitchen on my hands and knees. The noise was incredible. Viktor and Otto were fighting it out with enemies, who were firing from the kitchen door and window. But single shots from disciplined trigger squeezes on their MP40s were no match for the colossal incoming firepower. The heavy snaps of incoming rounds were constant, systematically disintegrating the kitchen and its fittings. Kitchen units splintered, glass cracked, crockery bursting everywhere. I felt a jab of weapon muzzle on my right buttock. I peered around. Thomas was glaring at me, face full of fury. "Get your fucking arse out of the way, you fool. Get to where you can fight!" But the kitchen was becoming untenable, even for Otto and Viktor. I kept low, scrambling and slipping across wet tiles until I reached the next room. Life would be short if you stood. Rounds kept snapping through, wall fittings bursting. All the blackout material was in shreds. I crawled over towards a window, my intention to fight from it. But a few feet short, the lower half of the window frame splintered and collapsed, causing the entire window, curtains and frame to crash down on top of me. The weight of it all stunned me, taking my breath. I was pinned to the floor, face down. The snaps of incoming fire grew even more intense. The Americans now had an entry point to the house, with me below it. I had to get out of the way, at least. I put the palms of my hands on the splinter and glass-littered floor, and began to push up. The frame began to shift; it wasn't as heavy as I thought, just fucking awkward. But suddenly, it doubled in weight, and I was pinned once more. A chattering of automatic fire directly above me had my ears ringing again. Searing hot brass hit the back of my head and neck. I tried to get my hands up to brush it away.

Once the gunfire directly over me ceased, my call for help was muffled, my hearing still gone. The weight on me lightened, the frame lifted from my body. Otto was stood over me, heaving the smashed frame away. "Don't just fucking lay there, boy, get out of the fucking way!" I crawled between his spread feet, away from the large hole that once held the frame. Once clear of him, I kneeled up. He dragged me by my shirt into the kitchen. The room was a wreck. The table was shattered. Behind it, Viktor was slumped against a unit beneath the sink. His eyes were still open, but there was no life in them. His blood hung like a spider web, all over a cupboard door. Otto clipped me around the head. "We cannot stay here!" he roared in my ear. There were still short controlled bursts from MG-42s upstairs. "We need to get to Detmold somehow!" It was broad daylight outside. Fighting our way through the Americans would be nothing short of suicide. But if we stayed in the house, we would certainly die. Another jarring thud hit the building. The Americans were throwing everything at us. Had they got armour out there? Or had they just walked in on Dieter's trail, carrying rockets?

Outside, I just made out a rather strange long roar. Then another. I smelt gasoline and burning wood. "Flamethrower!" screamed someone upstairs. The look of horror on Otto's' face was something I would never forget. Another long roar sounded. I coughed and spluttered as it took all the air, making me feel very ill and lightheaded. Upstairs, the short controlled bursts of machinegun fire became long and desperate; desperate men struggling to deal with the flamethrower menace. Each subsequent roar was accompanied by an overwhelming aroma of gasoline, and a horrendous amount of incoming fire. The Americans were protecting their best weapon, no doubt about it. Our own machinegun fire suddenly ceased, replaced by hysterical screaming. Otto waved for me to follow him. On our hands and knees, we scrambled back past the caved-in window in the next room, and into the corridor where I had first met Thomas. A staircase led upstairs, smoke thickly billowing from the upstairs rooms, filling an upstairs landing. A screaming mass of flame rushed out of a right-hand upstairs room, crashing into the banister, which tumbled, large clusters of flaming gasoline raining down. One of our gunners was amongst the flames. His screams went right through me. He hit the floor with such force, I heard his bones crunch. He spun around on the floor, like he was wrestling a crocodile or something, his screams becoming higher pitched. When I thought I couldn't take any more, a loud sharp snap rendered the human torch still.

It was only then I noticed the smoking Luger in Otto's hand. I was stunned beyond words. I knew why Otto had done it, but you never thought it would happen. "Let's get out of here!" he bellowed, as constant incoming snaps began to dismantle what was left of the staircase. I followed him in a crawl, back to the caved-in window. As he peered outside, I heard foreign voices echoing in the kitchen. Enemy troops had entered the house. They would not take pity on us. We had to flee. "Now!" hissed Otto, leaping to his feet. I followed him, scrambling through the opening. He was sprinting like a mad man for a log pile in an adjoining garden. I made off after him. We'd got about halfway there, when I heard shouting and commotion from the house. Multiple snaps passed us, splintering the log pile. Otto's torso burst in a fine red mist. He crashed to the floor face-first. I put more effort into my sprint, my lungs fit to burst as the snaps intensified. More tracer rounds flicked off the log pile, smashing into a nearby house. I slid in behind the logs, hugging the floor, my lungs burning. I dragged in air, like it was my last. Incoming fire thudded constantly into the log pile, which to my relief was fairly high with a wide base. Flicking tracer had set fire to a neighbouring roof. I was a heaving sweaty mess, in just a shirt, boots and trousers. I had no weapons left to defend myself, the window frame had seen to that. All I could do was sit tight, and pray the Americans wouldn't pursue me.

    The incoming fire into the logs lifted fairly quickly, but for sure, I couldn't stay there. I got up into a kneeling position, and slowly backed away. Over the top of the logs, I saw a big rising smoke column from the farmhouse we had been using. I slowly raised myself up. The house was a raging inferno. I knelt back down and turned away. I needed to get out of there, keeping out of the line of sight from the house. I knew there was a road between me and the other end of Berlebeck, various dwellings and outbuildings in between. Wire-strand fences would slow me down, but I would just have to dive over them. I made a short sharp dash behind the neighbouring house. Its roof fire had really taken hold now. Maybe the smoke would work in my favour.

I made a bold dash to the cobbled road. A stream just before it offered some cover, but not enough. I committed to crossing the road, dreading being fired on. I was yet again a heaving, lung-burning mess, by the time I made it to a cluster of houses on the other side. There was a lot more cover around me. I peered back down the road. The roof neighbouring the farmhouse had collapsed inwards. I just hoped no one was home.

I couldn't stick around too long. I couldn't see any Americans around the burning houses, but that didn't mean they weren't still in the area. Maybe their savage assault on the house was a revenge attack for the girl, and the guy we nailed to the logs. Or were the Americans simply advancing towards Detmold? I was sure I could make it there, once it got dark. But what would I do, once I got there? The locals might report me to the military police. The Americans could already be there. I didn't know of any family, or friends of my mother, living there. The locals would probably prefer not to assist or harbour a deserter; the authorities would be harsh on them, should I be discovered. There was a lot to risk in Detmold, but to be fair, living around here was risky. It quickly dawned on me that since my first venture into Berlebeck, I hadn't seen any locals. Was the place abandoned? Or were locals just hiding in their cellars? Besides the roaring and crackling of the burning buildings, nothing was going on. It would get dark quickly, the days were short. I wouldn't have to wait too long, before moving for Detmold. I was bloody cold, though.

I kept the cold at bay by constantly moving from house to house, trying to see if the enemy were still in the area. As the day wore on, the more I was convinced they had only stopped to destroy us. They had no need to sit in Berlebeck, longer than they had to. Thankfully, the light started to fade mid-afternoon, but the wind picked up, adding to my misery. I had to get moving soon. The sooner I got into Detmold, the sooner I would get food and warm clothing. I had to make up my mind whether to go through gardens and farmland, or stick to the roads. I had no map, so going through the fields could lead me to God knows where, but if I kept to the roads, military police might pick me up at a checkpoint. Labelled as a deserter, I would sooner take my chances with the Americans than our own side. Yes, the Americans could shoot me, but to be arrested by my own wasn't even worth considering. If what we did to the girl was anything to go by, Germany was in no mood to tolerate weak and defeatist people.

Chapter Sixteen – Horn

I couldn't stand hanging around any longer. I set off out of Berlebeck, hopefully in the right direction for Detmold. I took my chances on the roads, until I was clear of the village. If anything looked like a patrol, enemy or otherwise, I would just go to ground until they passed.

In open country, though, it became more difficult to consider getting away from the road; high hedgerows and deep ditches on either side. I began to hug the sides, but it made progress slow. I was losing light a lot faster than I expected. Spindly branches from a canopy above closed in, stealing the light. Every now and then, a gap in the hedgerows would reveal large gardens, chicken runs and wire-strand fences. I used the runs and gardens to stay off the road for a while, even though it slowed me down further. Little houses dotted the landscape. No lights, but the odd light-grey plume of smoke from a chimney. Every time I passed through a chicken run, I flinched if the chickens clucked from their little wooden houses. I was hungry, but taking care of one of them chickens was more trouble than it was worth. The racket one would make as I tried to grab it would wake half the neighbourhood. I would have had to carry it with me, and try to cook the thing somewhere suitable. The last time I ate meat was on the Senne, and that felt like a lifetime ago. My mind wandered to our classroom instruction there, a log fire roaring as the snow fell outside. The warm barrack block had a log-fire stove. But now look at me, in the back of beyond in just a fucking shirt, freezing my arse off. Max had been firm but fair, as instructors went. He had seen action in both France and Russia. He hadn't dazzled us with all that propaganda; stories many officers would lead you to believe. He would tell you exactly what combat was like, against the British and Russians. In France, he said the British were good fighters, but painfully slow and cautious. Many a time, his unit would get bored of waiting, and take the initiative to attack, as the British over-cautiously got their people into position. The Russians however were a totally different enemy. Extremely aggressive and mob-handed. They would throw unit after unit at any Germans facing them. Killing the Russians wasn't the problem, according to Max. It was having enough ammunition to kill all of them. His tank-killing prowess got him assigned to the Senne as an instructor. Wounded in both France and Russia, he recovered sufficiently to pass his knowledge on. I bet the last thing he planned was to be in the middle of a lesson one day, whilst receiving orders to march south with his students. To be brutally honest with myself, if it wasn't for what he taught me on the Senne, let alone what he taught me in the few hours before his death, I could very well be dead myself.

Open ground began to fall away on the right. I decided to cross it. The wire fences between the fields were a pain in the arse. Every time I tried to be quiet as I clambered over, the fences flicked like violin strings further down. It wasn't long before I was in a shallow valley of sorts, the road on high ground to my left. There was no traffic to be seen nor heard, but I was glad to be away from it, all the same. The absence of traffic reduced the chances of me running across a checkpoint of ours. The clouds began to part, and the moon lit up the whole area considerably. Navigation became easier. I started to anticipate the fences, and find a way of skirting around them. The only dilemma I had was the direction of my progress. With all my detours around fence lines, I didn't think I was getting any bloody closer to Detmold. The clear night made me all the more colder. My shirt had now dried to a certain extent, but it still didn't keep out the cold. The temptation to seek refuge in one of the houses was becoming all the more alluring, but the last time I broke into a house, I ended up with a load of SS deserters, claiming to do the Reichsfuhrer's bidding. As far as I was now concerned, they were just a bunch of thugs, trying to justify their existence. Some were likeable, let it be said, but they all had the same twisted ideas.

Before long, I was picking my way through small gardens; more dogs barking away, chickens and other livestock making silly noises. The racket had to be deemed as normal around here, since no one came out to investigate. I ended up on a loose gravel track. I tried to be as quiet as possible, but my boots made it difficult. The track took me about 200 metres or so, then I arrived at a main road. Not what I had planned, but then again, I had lost all sense of direction in the maze of gardens. Perhaps the road could help me reset my mental compass, but it was clear to me that I had somehow drifted back towards the road I had left. Oh well. I chose to walk on the road, until surroundings allowed me to divert again. It twisted and turned. The bends were long and shallow. I carefully paced my way around the long corners, making sure I didn't stumble across any soldiers, or civilians who might give me away. Civilians or soldiers, it might end badly for me. At the end of one bend, I noticed a road sign up ahead. I only made the sign out, once I was right on top of it. My heart sank.

'Welcome to Horn'

I so nearly cursed out loud. Erik, you fucking idiot, you are on the wrong road! The road I had discovered at the end of the gravel track was another road, branching off from one leading to Detmold. I was nowhere near fucking Detmold, but I knew where I was. In the grand scheme of things, I had almost walked in a huge circle. If I followed the right-hand road out of Horn, it would take me through Kohlstadt, and back to Schlangen. Not good. There was only one thing to do. Get into Horn and rest, then try again tomorrow for Detmold. I could feel myself getting all silly and emotional. I just wanted to eat, rest and get warm. I wanted to find a little place where I could just sit, and let the war pass me by. Call me a coward if you want, but it couldn't be much longer now, before the madness would finally end.

Horn was a much more cluttered village than Berlebeck. The houses almost sat on top of each other. No vast gardens to hide in. Plenty of damp log piles, and the like, but remaining hidden was going to be difficult, I could feel it. A long roadside ditch opened up to my right. I happily clambered into it, following it up the road.

Up ahead, I suddenly saw a lot of people and vehicle traffic. My stomach flipped. I hoped it wasn't a checkpoint. I heard shouting and cursing. As I slowly drew closer, I recognised the voices as German. Soldiers? SS? Police? Engine noise roared, and the unmistakable clattering of tracks. There was armour in Horn. To my right, there was a group of houses, scattered about a small hill of sorts. I got out of the ditch, and scuttled through small gardens. I did not want to get captured. In the darkness, it could be shoot first, check the body after. I carefully made my way to the top of a hill. The hill wasn't that big, but I had a decent view around. There were panzers down the other side. Lots of them parked up, almost nose to tail. Their crews were on them, or walking around. They appeared to be very relaxed, smoking away. One was playing an accordion, which I found alarming, as the Americans could very well be in the woods; you just couldn't tell. The hill was covered in thick trees, which gave me an element of cover. Away to my right, it sloped down to a road. I scanned the road for sentries; there were none. I needed to find somewhere to stay through the next day, somewhere I wouldn't be detected. But before I went looking for refuge, I needed to pee. Confident in my surroundings, I turned my back, and went about my business. I didn't have much to give, since I'd not drank anything for a while. "Hey you!" came a shout behind me. My whole world collapsed. "Hello," the voice shouted again, "you in the shirt." I dared not move. I heard crunches of leaf litter getting closer. I spun around. I was face-to-face with a soldier in full gear, who had a torch. "What are you playing at?" he demanded.

Playing at? I had no idea what he was suggesting. Possible explanations poured through my mind. I just had to front it out. "I'm taking a piss!" I boldly stated.

"Don't get funny with me, you scruffy buffoon!" barked the sentry. "The Hauptmann's orders are that all crew are correctly dressed, when away from their call signs."

Hauptmann? This had to be an army unit. Their rank structure was different to ours. "Oh, right," I said. "Sorry." I just couldn't think of anything else.

With a flick of his torch, he waved me down to the road. "Get back to your call sign. Don't fuck up again, understand?" The chance of me making a run for it was well and truly gone. If I had done so, army units would have been out in force, looking for one of their scruffy number, wearing just a shirt. My mind was racing. How the hell was I going to get out of this one? I walked down the hill, the sentry glaring at me all the way. There was a ditch just before the road. I jumped across, then made myself remotely presentable, tucking my shirt in properly, even ensuring my braces were over my shoulders. I ran my fingers through my hair, then set eyes on a crew, lounging all over a Panther. What the hell was I going to say to them? I couldn't say 'Hi, I'm Erik. I'm from the SS, and I'm looking to join your crew.' If they didn't beat me up on the spot, it would be a miracle. The army and SS never got on. I wasn't too sure why, perhaps a real professional rivalry. I had to play for time. I couldn't just climb on a vehicle. Tank crews were like families; you couldn't hide in their numbers. I decided to stroll to my right. The moon lit the area fairly well, but I hoped it was dark enough for me to buy some time, and think of something.

A crowd gathered ahead of me. "Everyone, get up here!" came a shout down the line. Oh shit. I eased off my confident stride, trying to think of a way I could get around the vehicles and vanish. What the hell was I going to do? I wasn't confident about my chances if they discovered an imposter amongst them. It might cause them a laugh to see the SS in a bad way, or it might spark outrage and a lynch mob. All around, panzer crews clambered down from their vehicles. The waft of tobacco smelt amazing. Farts and coffee breath soon mixed in with the aroma of unwashed men. I found myself in amongst a loose crowd. I heard a gallop of boots behind me, as further tank crews caught up. Darkness would only be my friend for so long. It would soon be a new day. What that day would bring was anyone's guess. I was in the middle of a large group of strangers. Any fear of the situation suddenly evaporated. If I aroused suspicion, I would introduce myself to their commander, who would hopefully keep the mob at bay. After all, they would want every man capable of fighting, surely? We drew up just in front of what appeared to be a group of officers. Even in the low light, I could tell all was not well. Some of the officers were sobbing quietly, some openly. Some had hands on hips, looking up at the dark sky, shaking their heads. The only one who looked unfazed was one in the middle, slowly and carefully folding up his map. He invited us all to smoke with him, whilst he addressed us. He rolled himself a cigarette. The glow of his match gave away that he had not shaven in a while. I carefully scanned about me. It was evident that most others hadn't shaved recently. I didn't feel so scruffy. The unfazed officer asked the troops to sit down. Most just slumped where they had stood. I carefully squatted down low. The officers remained standing. I peered around again. Some of the more grizzled veterans, who must have been NCOs, remained standing at the rear.

The officer in the middle cleared his throat. "Gentlemen, it appears that events have overtaken us, in a way I never ever once considered. Germany is in trouble. Real trouble. By rights, I should keep you focused on your mission to fight for your Fuhrer, your Fatherland, and your way of life. But I feel that to do so, I would be nothing more than a fraud." Mutters and murmurs slowly built up. He held out his hands for calm. "I must now be open and frank with you. Not as your Commanding Officer, but as a fellow man caught up in these circumstances that we are party to. When I took command of this unit just prior to Poland, it was one of the greatest feelings in my entire life, second only to the birth of my children. I felt invincible. Poland, Belgium, Holland, France, I felt as if nothing could stop my boys." He was starting to well up. But he composed himself well, clearing his throat again. "And then there was Russia. Russia beat us up really bad. A lot of good boys were lost in Russia, and if I was brutally honest with you, it gave me sleepless nights. I began to live in fear of losing more the next day, for more land than any man could possibly want. Kursk almost cost me everything. Our losses were horrendous. The powers that be saw fit to return us to France for rest and refitting, and I won't lie to you men, that was some of the greatest news I had heard in a while." Again, he was trying his hardest not to break down. Even some of the hard-faced NCOs were putting up a good fight with the tears. "Last year turned out to be the bloodiest year I have ever witnessed. Normandy was a tough fight, but we managed to get out of France. The Hurtgenwald is where most of you sat before me cut your teeth. I'm proud to say you guys gave a good account of yourselves there. We struggled to get fuel and spares, but we made it work. I am eternally grateful for the job you did in the Hurtgen." In front of me in the crowd, nods accompanied shoulder patting. "Now let's talk about where we are now. We have no fuel, no spares. And little, if any ammunition. We have not had contact with command for some time now. We know that there is a substantial American force in Paderborn. And up north towards Minden, there are British units pushing east. So as you can guess, we are in a bit of a fix. I have spoken to my officers just a few minutes ago, and I have made it clear that I will no more order you into a fight, where the odds are stacked against us. As of now, my obligation to you is to see that you leave the battlefield alive. As of now, you are free to return to your homes, or find other units in the area. You have served your country, and served it well. Now I must, as an officer, and as a man endeavouring to save your lives, for I have lost enough since 1939, say enough is enough." There was stunned silence. I was stunned. Never did I think I would hear an officer speak this way. It was a bizarre feeling. We could all walk away now, without reprisal. He cleared his throat again, wiping away tears. "Sentries! I would be eternally grateful if you don't shoot any member of my unit who wishes to leave. Thank you." He looked over us, eyes glazed, a broad warm smile on his face. "Go home, boys, go home. Consider a handshake with your former Commanding Officer the end of your contract." He walked over to the front of the column, and rolled himself another cigarette. His officers slowly made their way towards him. Some joined him in a smoke. Others just stood there, hands in pockets, playing with the gravel beneath their boots. He shook all their hands. Some burst into tears, thanking him for letting them go home. It was totally bizarre; a unit disbanded in the field. Would the SS do such a thing? Probably not. The lads around me slowly got to their feet, some tearful. Many began shaking hands with those around them. Others remained seated, totally numb.

We could all go home.

I kept myself to myself, as the boys around me, mostly young but some older, embraced each other, sobbing openly. It truly was a wonderful day for them. As far as fighting was concerned, their war was over. Their next risky adventure was getting home. For most, it would be difficult. For some, it would end in heartbreak. Their families were fighting the war as well. The boys from the cities knew the enemy had destroyed most things there. God only knew what they would find, upon their return. They would have to brave the military police checkpoints, and any other units on their path home. And then there was the enemy. Getting rounded up as prisoners was a real possibility too. Did they go home armed, since they might need to defend themselves? Or did they lay down their arms, and take their chances? Getting home; it was still all to play for.

But there was not the mass exodus I expected. Most of the boys took their weapons back to their tanks; some old habits would forever die hard. As scruffy as the boys appeared, they had kept their tank column immaculate. They seemed in no rush to leave, probably contemplating the long journey home. I felt for those from the east, some of their home towns overrun by the Russians. The tank crews just lounged about on their vehicles again; laughing, smoking and making coffee, some singing along to the accordion.

I felt the presence of someone. I turned to see their Commanding Officer. "They are good boys," he muttered, looking off into the distance, letting out a long pillar of cigarette smoke. "I just couldn't send them to their deaths anymore."

I was bang to rights, so I just played along. "Yes sir."

He turned to look at me. I noticed he wasn't particularly tall. In the growing light of dawn, I could see his dark hair swept back, his face carrying several days of beard. He was handsome, but had a piercing, confident glare, which you would expect from an officer of the Wehrmacht. "I know almost all of my men, but I'm afraid you have me at a loss, young man. I'm Erik Wrobel." He held out his hand with a beaming smile.

I accepted his hand. "Erik Baum, sir."

His grip was firm, very firm. "Handsome name there, Erik, your parents made a great choice." He released his grip. The blood washed back into my hand. "Where are you from, young Erik?"

"Paderborn, sir. Bad Lippspringe."

He nodded slowly. "I didn't know we had any Paderborn boys in the unit." I suddenly felt fear flood through me. "I'm surprised you were not recruited into the SS," he added.

I did not want to betray a man who had just allowed his men to go home, so I tried to come clean. "Sir, my unit was destroyed but a few days ago, just south of Kohlstadt. I have been evading the Americans ever since, and I stumbled across your unit, quite by accident this morning."

He crossed his arms, and stroked his beard. "So that would be the tank fire we heard. My orders were to link up with an SS outfit, just south of here. But you SS guys can be a prickly bunch to work with, let it be said. We were so low on fuel and ammunition, I decided not to link up, and commit my boys to a bloodbath. I'm sure you understand."

His was the unit sent to reinforce us. My thoughts became filled with Max, Bobby and Marco. I nodded. "Sir, that one act has saved the lives of so many of these guys. The Americans threw everything at us. It would have been a waste of life."

He nodded, continuing to stroke his beard. "Agreed. At least these boys can go home. I'm tired, Erik. We are merely playing for time now. How many more have to die, before it all stops?"

He had become a little animated. I swallowed hard. I had to ask him. "Sir, may I go home too?"

He looked me straight in the eyes. "My young Erik, even the SS have mothers, so I'm told." His cheeky wink reassured me that I was not about to be handed over to another unit. "Go home, but be cautious. The Americans are a prickly bunch too. Very unpredictable, take it from me."

A feeling of joy rose up in me, to a point I could feel my eyes flooding. I shook his hand vigorously with both of mine. "Thank you, sir, thank you."

I could go home.

Chapter Seventeen: The End of the Road

The tank crews still weren't going anywhere. I almost felt that none of them wanted to be the first to shake the Commanding Officer's hand, and walk away. Maybe as far as they were concerned, they were home. By the look of them, they had been to hell and back together, just to see how far it was. The panzer commander of one crew, the oldest among them, was almost playing mother hen. They were his children in a sense. He refilled their coffee cups, lit their cigarettes. Playing cards was the main activity on the turret. Other crews just laid around smoking, some reading books. There were even a few, quite literally sleeping on their engine decks. I envied them all in a way. I hadn't been in the military long enough to really bond with a unit. The events of the last few days had really messed things up. I could only hazard a guess where some of the other guys from my old Senne barrack block were now. If they were not already prisoners, they would probably be dead. Such a waste of youth.

I had to plan my route home. I would make my way carefully into Kohlstadt. With a bit of luck, the Americans hadn't reached it yet. If they had, I would have to get past them somehow. It would be a dangerous route. The Americans could well be in the mood to shoot at anything that moved.

I made my way to the front of the column. The Commanding Officer was leaning over the bonnet of a Kubelwagon, studying a map. I stood waiting for him to finish, but my presence caught his eye. "Young Erik, you still here?" His face was all smiles.

I held out my hand. "I wanted to thank you again for letting me go, sir."

He received it with both of his. "Erik, go home. You were never under my command in the first place. Besides, these goons are not in a rush to leave, so I will stay to see them off." He released his iron grip, and went back to his map.

My curiosity got the better of me. "Where is home for you, sir?"

"Seelow." He slowly turned to face me. My blank expression gave away that I had no clue where Seelow was. "In the east, perhaps in Russian hands," he added, peering back down at the map.

I felt such a fraud, being literally on the doorstep of my hometown. "I'm sorry, sir."

He looked at me with a stern gaze. "Erik, what have you got to be sorry for? You didn't create this mess. None of us here did. But it's us that must pay for it. History will not be kind to Germany, you do realise that? We will all pay dearly for what has happened in the last six years. So much suffering, and for what? Look where it has got us, Erik." His eyes were glazed, his lips trembling. I was starting to feel uncomfortable. He stood up straight, reached out, and put a gentle hand on my shoulder. "Erik, you must ensure you get home safely. Promise me. I would like to at least have done some good in this awful war." He was starting to lose it.

I tried to nod convincingly. "I promise, sir." Now it was me, trying to hold it together.

He broke into a broad, tight-lipped grin, which caused the dam to break, tears rolling down his cheeks. "Go, Erik. Be careful how you get past the Americans. Like I said, they are unpredictable." I shook his hand once more, and turned away. As I moved away from the column, I was suddenly overwhelmed with loneliness. The boys in the column were with family of sorts. My guess was that they were just waiting for the Americans to take them into custody.

I followed the road to Kohlstadt. It was early dawn now, making it easier to see the village in the distance. It was in a kind of gorge. I was cold, but that was the least of my concerns. I wanted to get home. In just shirt, trousers and boots, there was nothing to indicate I was SS. That could well go in my favour, if watching Americans decided I was just a wandering soldier. I decided to remain on the main road. All was quiet, nothing to be overly concerned about. As I made my way towards the outskirts, I saw white bed sheets, fluttering from almost every window. The residents clearly had no desire to resist the invader, and who could blame them? You would be forgiven if you had the feeling the war was starting to ease off. I began to pass houses. They were immaculate, gardens all picture-perfect. The war had not ruined this town. The bed sheets were all brilliant white. Everything was perfect. I just hoped Bad Lippspringe still looked like a postcard.

I was almost halfway through Kohlstadt, when I detected movement up ahead. My stomach turned over, as I looked desperately for somewhere to hide. I leapt into gardens on my left, and crawled behind bushes close to the footpath. I peered through, and to my relief, some women were pulling an empty cart along. Their children were running, jumping, and skipping around their feet. I felt it wise to let the women pass, not too confident of their mood. They might have been friendly to me, or they might have reported me to the nearest American unit, who knew? They went past, going about their business. I emerged back onto the path, and continued on my way.

I was almost at the southern end of town, when I made out the rooftops of Schlangen. I knew first-hand that the Americans were in Schlangen, or at least were the other day. Fortunately,

Bad Lip sat just south of the village, behind it and to the left, from where I was looking. Off to my right was lots of open farmland. I could venture out wide and go round Schlangen. I moved off the road, through gardens and clucking chickens again, and the usual yapping bloody dog, then out through the hedgerows and ditches. As I carefully picked my way through the fields, my mind started to wander. Every time I used a wire-strand fence to get my bearings, I saw the girl. We hadn't been forced to kill her. That bastard Dieter enjoyed it, no doubt. If there was a Dieter in every village and town filled with enemy, Germany would be a very dark place, for some time to come. It couldn't be long now, before the war was over. One way or another, the killing must end soon, surely.

The route was painfully slow, but vital. I couldn't afford to drift near Schlangen. What suddenly filled me with dread was the thought that if Schlangen was still occupied by the Americans, then Bad Lip must be. I had not considered it until now. But there wasn't much I could do about it. Should I wait 'til dark? Take my chances then? I clambered onto a fence to get a feel for my whereabouts. Schlangen was off to my left now. I was confident if I continued on a little bit further, I could then strike a straight line into Bad Lip. Not far now, Erik, just don't rush it. Getting through hedges and over fences became more difficult. Brambles ripped my shirt badly. Every so often, I spent a couple of minutes, picking myself free from thorns. I began to perspire, which at least kept the cold at bay. There was a break in the clouds. The

Sun beamed through, feeling fantastic on my face. In the far distance, it glimmered on little lakes, which sat on the outskirts of my neighbourhood. It was like a mirage in the desert. So close, Erik, so close. I took my time to scan the ground ahead, for anything that might cause a problem, especially Americans. I saw nothing. Had they moved further into Germany? Were some of their units hunkered down in Bad Lip? I couldn't tell. But from what I could make out, there was no evidence of fighting in my hometown. No burning houses; they looked in good shape. I could make out white bed sheets, flapping from upstairs windows. No fighting here, please. As I scanned further to my left, I could see Paderborn still smouldered. Such a beautiful city. I hoped she could be fixed, after all the nonsense was over.

Happy, I pressed towards home. I made sure I didn't rush into anything. Being cautious was good, but it made progress outrageously slow. With all my willpower, I fought the urge to break into a childish sprint, and run straight to my front door. For a while, the lakes didn't seem to get closer. Between them was a narrow strip of land. I used to play around the lakes, but a couple of years ago. Willi and Manfred would take me there, when they had leave. We would swim. I missed Willi. Such a waste. I just hoped Manfred had been in touch with mother. I was sure there were thousands of families all over Germany, fretting over loved ones. It wasn't just those who went to fight that were fretted over, since the war was now in our streets, so to speak. It engulfed everyone. It must surely be over soon.

Before long, I was just short of the lakes. I could almost see the roof of my house, in the streets behind. I felt going between the lakes was unwise. Should I draw attention to myself, I would be restricted on where I could run. I decided to go around them, taking a route to my left. It would keep me in the fields, whereas the right-hand route would take me close to the houses. As I made my way around the lakes, I anxiously tried to locate my house. I paused behind some bushes, and got a grip of myself. I should be looking out for the enemy, not the fucking chimney stack of my home.

After moving around the lakes, I carefully made my way through the first row of houses. Nothing suspicious; neat and tidy, white bed sheets out in force. As I picked my way through gardens, I noticed it was strangely quiet. Nothing out of the ordinary, but I was used to getting the shit scared out of me by snapping dogs or clucking chickens. I just needed to get through the next row of gardens, to get to my street. The properties around my house backed onto each other. Don't rush it, Erik. My heart almost failed, when a baby suddenly started crying. I suddenly felt sick, and had to sit down to compose myself. I was in my neighbour's alleyway. I felt I should at least smarten myself up a bit. I tucked my shirt in, and made sure my trousers hung properly, my braces untwisted. I rubbed my boots on the backs of my thighs to bring on a shine. Why on Earth I felt it all necessary was anyone's guess; old habits, I suppose. I peered out into my street, confident there wasn't an American armoured column, having a street party. I took in the scene. Besides the white bed sheets, all looked as I remembered it, when I went off for basic training. Beautiful. I felt a lump rise up in my throat. You are home, Erik. I politely and quietly walked out into my street, my home now in full view. Still nice and tidy, just how mother liked it. I made my way through my garden, and stopped just short of the front door. Our front door sat at the side of the house, opposite our neighbour's door. The doors were almost a mirror image of each other. Mine was on the left. I suddenly felt like a stranger. Should I ring the bell? Knock on the door? Or just walk straight in? I dismissed bounding straight in, not wanting to give my mother a heart attack. She must be using all the bed sheets, since every upstairs window had one flapping from it. I closed my eyes, clenched my fist, leaned forward and knocked. Why is it when you knock on a door, those few waiting seconds feel like the longest ever? I was suddenly overwhelmed with worry that she had fled the fighting, and could be anywhere. I knocked again. I made out the clatter of shoes on our tiled foyer floor. The top bolt crashed across, then the bottom one. The main handle began to turn, the door creaked open. Silver hair, tied up in a bun, appeared around the door. Her eyes squinted as she adjusted to the light. Her little face came into full view. I had only been here last, but a few weeks ago on leave. It felt like a lifetime. She looked at me warily. Her face suddenly changed, when she realised the scruffy half-dressed soldier at her door was in fact her youngest son. "Erik?" Her voice was quiet and gentle. I nodded, wanting to speak, but my voice failed me. The door opened wider. She stepped over the threshold, holding her little hands out. I took her hands in mine. Her hands were so small, yet very rough to the touch. Mother was never one for pampering herself, at the best of times. Her eyes glazed instantly, dams on the verge of breaking. I couldn't keep myself together. I welled up. Her small hand stroked my cheek. "My little Erik," she croaked. "I thought I had lost all my boys." I kissed her hand. I felt like a little boy in a big, bad man's world. She stepped forward, and embraced me around my midriff. She wasn't very tall. I pushed my tear-soaked face into her hair. I could smell soap, fresh and clean. I didn't want to let go of her. Her shoulders bounced, as she sobbed into my chest. We stayed there for ages, attached to each other. I was home. Home appeared to be in one piece. I was so grateful to the Americans, for not turfing my mother out into the river of refugees fleeing the fighting. I silently thanked our own masters, for not making a stand in these streets. The only sound nearby was the fluttering of bed sheets.

She released her tight embrace and looked up at me. "Is it over, Erik?"

"I don't know," I admitted, "I really don't know."

She took a step back, wiping the palms of her hands over her tear-streaked face. "I so want it to be over, Erik, this madness has gone on for too long."

I nodded, wanting to think the entire country had tired of it. There was a risk of upsetting her, but I had to ask. "Anything from Manfred?"

She shook her head. "Nothing. Last letter I had, he was in Russia, and that was before you went to basic training." Russia was so vast, you could lose another country in there. I had a feeling he died long ago, but wouldn't dare advance my theory to her. Losing Willi in France shattered her. I had to at least let her grip onto the hope Manfred could still be out there somewhere, trying to get home. She reached forward, taking my hands again, eyeing me up and down. "You look terrible, Erik." She slowly shook her head in disapproval.

"Thanks," I chuckled. The mood felt much lighter. She turned to enter the house, waving me inside.

"I will run you a bath, so you can get out of those filthy clothes." She swivelled to look at me, but her face turned to horror. "ERIK!"

I didn't see or hear it coming. As the world swam back into focus, my head throbbed outrageously. I could hear muffled shouting and screaming. My pain became more acute, as I gathered myself. I was flat on my back, my right ear cold on the floor tiles. I lifted my heavy head, and what greeted me was something I had never imagined. My mother was on her knees, her face bleeding and bruised. A soldier stood over her, his hand gripping her hair roughly, as he struck her across the face. He went to strike her again, but hesitated, and dropped her like a sack. He span around to glare at me. Thomas' eyes were full of hate. "You thought you could just run away, you little fuck!" he roared, stampeding towards me. I lifted my knees up to my chest, as I scrambled backwards. I could only go so far, since the cellar stairs were directly behind me. He grabbed my flesh through my shirt. Pain screamed through my body. He grabbed my hair with his other hand, ripping me up from the floor, hauling me back towards mother and the front door. She scrambled to her feet to bar his way, but he raised his right boot. He ploughed it into her face with all his strength, her face bursting in red mist, as her tiny inert frame crumpled.

I roared into his face. "You fucking bastard, you dare touch my mother?"

I was cut short, as his forehead smashed into the bridge of my nose. My world faded, sparkles all over the place. He released his grasp, allowing gravity to take care of me. "Silence, you cowardly turd!" he spat at me. "First, I'm going to string up this Jewish whore, then I'm going to have fun with you." As he went to grab mother, her little hand went up in protest. He flicked it away, dealing a blow to her head. Her whole body went limp. I clambered to my feet, as he turned to confront me. I rhino-charged him, full on in the gut. He let out an almighty grunt, as I took the air from his lungs. We both crashed into the doorframe, my head in the wrong place, taking the majority of the impact. The sparkles returned. I ran out of steam quickly, as he got the better of me. He shoved me back. I went top heavy, staggering back, as I tried to stay on my feet. The hard stone doorstep took my feet from me, and I crashed against the door. Before I could react, he was on top of me, pinning me down, hands clasped tight around my throat. I grabbed his wrists, and with all that remained of my strength, I tried to prise them away. He was not a small man, solid and powerful. He was well on his way to squeezing the life out of me. I began losing feeling in my hands, my whole world fading once more. The pressure around my neck was overwhelming. I just couldn't summon the strength to break his grip.

But then the pressure disappeared, accompanied by an ear-splitting thud. He suddenly went limp, all his weight bearing down on me. I couldn't catch my breath. He coughed and gargled in my face. I rocked left and right, trying to get some leverage to push him away. I managed to heave him off me, his head slamming down on the doorstep, as he rolled away outside. Life and air rushed back into my lungs. I took in great gulps, coughing uncontrollably with each intake of the precious air. He was on his back, head propped up by the step, mouth full of blood, bubbling every red breath down his chin. His breathing was shallow, his eyes open and bloodshot. I was overwhelmed by an aroma of human shit, and strong urine. I was confident it wasn't me. I wasn't too sure about him. I rolled away from him, onto my side. My head still spun, like I had been drunk. I propped myself up on my right elbow, and saw mother slumped, face bloodied and bruised. In her lap, still smoking, was a Mauser rifle. Standard military issue. She had taken care of Thomas. She was tougher than she looked.

I sat upright. My legs would not respond to my wishes, my head swimming. I must have looked pathetic, as I crawled over to my bloodied and broken mother. She tossed the rifle to one side. My head drew level with her thighs. A little rough hand cupped my left ear. She invited me to rest my battered head in her lap. I tried to be polite, but ended up with the entire weight of my head and shoulders on her. Exhaustion was getting the better of me. When I was little, just before bedtime, my brothers and I would sit in front of the fire with her, all of us bathed and clean. Me being the youngest, I would have my head in her lap, and she would play with my ear. I found it so relaxing, I would drift off. She would then cart me up to bed, without me realising it. And now, with her little hand stroking my ear, I felt so at peace.

Spluttering and gargling from Thomas distracted me from my slumber. I tried to lift my head to look at him, but she wouldn't allow it. "Shush," she soothed in my ear, "let him go."

He was in a bad way. The bullet must have smashed his spine, since he could only move his torso. Blood around his lower back and buttocks was dark, starting to congeal and dry. He was trying to reach behind him, but paralysed from the waist down, he couldn't do it. All he could do was lay in his own shit and piss, and allow life to drain out of him. With a gargle and a splutter, he drew his elbows alongside his chest, and clumsily propped himself up, fixing us a hateful stare. "It's because of weak people like you, Germany is in this position," he managed to gasp.

I went to bark back at him, but mother placed a gentle hand over my mouth. "You are right, my dear," she whispered gently to him. "For allowing men like you to lead Germany into this position." His glare suddenly dropped. He hadn't banked on such a quick answer from a battered little woman. In sheer contempt, he spat blood at us, and slumped back. Groaning began to accompany his gargling, but he refused to die. I felt my mother's little fingers running through my filthy matted hair. "Let's get you cleaned up," she whispered to me. Remarkable; this little woman had almost been killed, and her only concern was sorting me out. I lifted my delicate head from her lap. She managed to get herself to her feet, and then helped me up. I still felt a bit unsteady.

"Woman!" gargled Thomas. "Since I doubt your boy is up to it, feel free to end my war for me."

I just wanted to finish him off, but mother grasped my arm. She told me to stay where I was. She stepped through the doorway, towards his foul frame. Ensuring she was out of his reach, she knelt down next to him. "What is your name, young man?" she said gently.

He glared at her. "What the fuck has that got to do with anything?"

She remained passive. "What harm could it do, to be properly introduced?"

His glare relaxed slightly. "Thomas, my name is Thomas."

She stood up, smiling and courteous. "Well, let me tell you what we are all going to do now, Thomas. We are going to sit tight, including you, and wait for this horrible war to be over."

As she stepped away from him, and closed the door, we were subject to his last defiant gesture. "You fucking Jewish whore!"

With the door shut, the foyer was dark. She shuffled to a lamp. The soft glow gave off an amazing feeling of homeliness and warmth. "What do we do now?" I asked.

She smiled. "We wait for the Americans. There is nothing else we can do."

And the Americans did arrive eventually, but not for me. I remained upstairs, when the knock at the door came. I peered through nets that covered the window, and saw an American patrol in the street. Thomas had been down there for about two days. I don't think he made it through the first night. The American in charge talked through an interpreter; a captured German soldier. Mother explained that she thought Thomas had been shot by an American patrol. She had been too scared to go out and investigate. Through the interpreter, the American asked how she obtained her facial injuries. She told them she fought off some looters. The American appeared satisfied with her explanation. He called up a big truck to take Thomas away.

Whilst I enjoyed my first bath that evening, at home in front of the fire, mother took what was left of my uniform, and put it on the fire. The only things that refused to burn were the hobnails on the soles of my boots. I had a few baths that evening, since the grime coating me was unrelenting. Once I was clean, and dressed in loose shirt and trousers, mother and I tended to our wounds. We would both recover. Her broken nose was the only substantial injury sustained. Being at home was a great feeling, but also one of nervousness. I kind of expected Americans to do house searches, looking for hiding soldiers. I wondered if the SS or our military police would come into town, to enforce their policies upon us.

Mother insisted I stay indoors for the foreseeable future, since no one actually knew if the war was over. I was of fighting age, and could well be interned. Fighting age, that was a joke in itself. In those last weeks of the war, if you could fire a weapon, you were of fighting age. Germany's source of fighting men was hardly vast in 1945, let it be said. Food was a problem, since the Americans had to not only feed their armies and prisoners, but were tasked with helping the civilian population from the brink of starvation. For some time, potatoes and vegetables were the staple diet. Bread wasn't too hard to come by, thankfully many people made their own. Mother's bread was only satisfactory, but it did the job. I can't exactly remember when meat arrived back on the menu. The Americans didn't stay too long in Bad Lip. They soon moved further into Germany, a clear indicator the war was not over just yet.

I remember one afternoon, mother came in, and called me downstairs. She was full of smiles. The German army had formerly surrendered. A huge wave of relief washed over me. Yes, it was clear we had been defeated, but it meant there would be no more fighting. I went out into the street. The white sheets still fluttered like flags, but to be outside again was an awesome feeling. The street was very quiet. Losing the war was not a cause for celebration, but I deny anyone, German or otherwise, wasn't happy the fighting had ended.

Epilogue: After the Madness

Over the next few months, mother was happy and sad in equal measure. The former fighting men of Germany were being released, and were coming home. Slowly, men from Bad Lip, and the Paderborn area in general, were present on the streets once more. They had been taken prisoner by the British, Americans, French and Canadians. The boys from Russia had not yet returned. I heard of some men talking about working in America as farm labourers. No fences, no watchtowers, just the middle of America. My thoughts drifted back to those still in Russia. Was Manfred amongst them? I would have given anything for my mother to receive a letter, confirming he was alive. Not knowing was the worst part of all.

Paderborn was in a real bad way. Her rail yard and roads were shattered beyond recognition. Unless you were skilled in building or engineering, you probably wouldn't have a job there. Unemployment was a big problem, for some time after the war. We had food, that wasn't a problem, but money was very hard to come by. Just to get me out of the house, I volunteered to work in Paderborn, clearing out the wrecked areas. As trite as it may seem, my job was to collect intact bricks, and stack them on the back of a horse-drawn cart. They would be used in the rebuild, whenever that happened. Unexploded bombs were a risk in Paderborn, and there were some tragedies. I was soon offered a job as a farm labourer, just outside Schlangen. The money wasn't movie star wages, but mother and I were grateful for it, all the same.

Years passed before the first boys from Russia were released. They were empty shells of men. They looked terrible, old before their time, because of hard labour in Siberia. I wouldn't ask for sympathy, regarding how they were treated. We had much to be ashamed of during those dark years. Mother would approach the men as they waited for buses, or drank coffee in cafes. There were thousands of them around. I felt her efforts for them were all in vain, but I couldn't bring myself to tell her. If Manfred wasn't dead, there was still a chance.

Over the years, we began to see an improvement in Paderborn. I was so grateful Bad Lip had not been mauled by the fighting. I continued working on the farm. Wages got a little better. Mother became less active.

I returned home from work one evening. Mother was at our large table in the kitchen, tears streaming down her face. She kept kissing a letter, rubbing her cheek with it. She looked up at me with a face full of smiles, her cheeks smeared in ink, unable to speak. All she did was wave the letter at me, imploring me to read. It had a Red Cross letterhead. As I tried my best to read around the smears, it became apparent her prayers had been answered. Manfred was alive. He was in Berlin under medical and nutritional supervision, and would be arriving at Paderborn Hauptbahnhof in the next few days. I burst into tears, as my not so frail mother sprung to her feet and embraced me. Thank you, thank you, thank you.

It was great to have Manfred home. He looked a little rough around the edges, and certainly underweight, but apart from that, it was fantastic to have him back. My boss on the farm gave me a day off to spend time with Manfred, and even gave me a few small bottles of beer. What a nice guy my boss was. Once mother and I had eaten with Manfred, and she had kissed us both goodnight, we settled down with the beers, telling each other of our adventures. My tales were rather tame in comparison to his. I didn't tell him about the girl, or the crucified American. As far as Manfred was concerned, I escaped from an American artillery bombardment, and joined a unit in Horn. His stories were far more chilling. What he told me about Russia confirmed what Bobby had told me in Kirchborchen. Manfred's stories of Siberia made me uncomfortable. The Russians hadn't wasted trucks and fuel on prisoners. Prisoners walked everywhere. Anyone that couldn't keep up was shot on the spot. Once Manfred's group reached their prison camp area, they had to build the camp themselves. They were frozen and starving. Their captors threw axes and saws in the snow, and told them to find building materials. There was a forest about a kilometre away, so the prisoners dragged felled trees to use for the build. It took weeks, hundreds perishing in the snow. There was no wire fence around the perimeter. The Russians hadn't felt the need, as there was nothing in any direction. My war had lasted merely days, so I felt a bit of a fraud. We talked about Willi. He had been killed at a place called Falaise, that's all I knew. Over the years, I have read many history books about the Battle of Normandy. Falaise was the epicentre of destruction for the German army in France. The only units to make it out of France were badly mauled. By the time it came to fight in Paderborn, our army was little more than older men and young boys, fighting with some experienced officers and NCOs. They were all expected to go on and win the war, defeating everything they encountered on all fronts in Germany. Total madness. If anything had been learnt from the war, it had to be a warning to those who might choose to follow the beliefs of one bitter and twisted man, since more than likely, they would follow such a man into chaos.

Time marches on. Today, mother is no longer with us. Manfred also passed away, not too long ago. My children now have their own children. How Germany has changed. Full of promise again, but not in a menacing way. As a nation, we are an economic force. We have our issues, same as most other countries; the EU, immigration. My sons completed their national service in the Bundeswehr. They hated it, but finished their basic training. One of them went peacekeeping in Somalia, the other did pretty much the same in Kosovo. My grandchildren are taught about the Holocaust at school. The Holocaust is something we must not be allowed to forget, but I do feel sorry for our teenagers these days. People like to ram it down their throats, when it suits them. Don't blame our grandchildren, blame their grandparents; we are the ones to blame. On the news now and then, we hear of some war criminal being arrested in South America, or somewhere exotic like that. If I may be so bold as to make an observation, the main ringleaders of all that was terrible, all that time ago, are now long dead. It appears to me that those groups who dedicate their lives to tracking people down are now clutching at straws. Just because an old man manned a watchtower as a boy, it does not make him a murderer of innocents.

But every night I go to bed, I think of the girl.

Every night, I fear the Nazi hunters.

Printed in Great Britain
by Amazon.co.uk, Ltd.,
Marston Gate.